THE HEART BREAKER

CATHRYN FOX

ISBN Ebook: 978-1-989374-43-6

ISBN Print: 978-1-989374-42-9

DECLAN

Christmas Eve:

Tension radiates off my buddy, Brody, and fills the interior of his sports car as he eases it into my parents' slippery driveway. I tear my gaze away from all the twinkling lights on the snow-covered shrubs, worry going through me as I take in my friend's deep frown. Man, it's been a hell of a week off—for both of us.

It was just last month I invited Brody to come to my home-town of Holiday Peak, Massachusetts, to spend Christmas with my family and me. As soon as we got here, we set up a stupid bet that involved the local chocolatier, and in the end, my buddy went and fell for the girl who seemed to have a hate on for him. Tonight? Well, tonight was all about him trying to make things right with her, and while I was more than happy to help him—hell, I want to see him happy—I hated being away from my girl Nikki Walsh for one single second.

Technically, she's not my girl. Nikki and I have been best friends since kindergarten—she's the only girl we allowed into our treehouse—and because I now live in Boston and play for the Seattle Shooters, we rarely get to see each other, and yes, it's possible that I'm in love with her and too chicken shit to do anything about it.

But fuck, man, she means everything to me, and while we joke and carry on, she's honestly giving me whiplash. One minute I think she wants to take things further, the next she's colder than the snowman on my neighbor's lawn. I'm afraid of making a move and ruining everything we've built over the years. I'd rather be her friend than run the risk of losing her. Yeah, that's right. Chicken shit.

"You good, bro?" I ask Brody, and he nods, but he's not good. He needs to do some serious damage control to win back his girl's trust.

He exhales loudly and stares straight ahead, a little lost in thought. "Yeah, I think I need a good night's sleep."

I study his face as the dashboard light highlights deep lines around his eyes. "The party should have died down by now," I tell him. There's only one car left on the street, which is a good indication that Mom's annual Christmas Eve dinner party has ended.

"Good, I'm not in the mood to talk to anyone." He kills the engine, grips the steering wheel, and shakes his head. "Sorry for tearing you away from the party, and from Nikki. I know you don't get enough time with her as it is, and here I am dragging you into my shit."

"I wouldn't have it any other way." I open my door and a cool winter breeze swirls around the interior of the car. "We'd better get inside. She's going to need a drive home." I step from the vehicle and my heart speeds up a bit. It's insane how excited I am to see her. I've only been gone a little over an hour, yet I can't wait to have her close. I know I can't touch or kiss her like I want, but I can throw my arm around her—under the guise that she might slip on the icy driveway, of course—as I walk her to my car and see her home safely. I grin. Maybe this year under the mistletoe, she'll actually kiss me instead of whacking my chest and laughing. Heck, maybe I'll finally get that kiss on New Year's Eve when the ball drops.

Brody and I are supposed to head back to Boston right after Christmas, but I always try to come back for the big New Year's bash. No one does the holidays quite like the folks here in Holiday Peak. Over the top decorations and parties? Hell yeah. Would I want it any other way? Nope.

Brody lags as I dart up the stairs and open the front door, and my heart sinks when I glance into the living room to find Mom, Dad and Aunt Jeannie. Mom takes one look at me and frowns. She stands, and crosses the room.

"Declan, what is it?"

I glance past her shoulder and turn around to see into the kitchen. "Where's Nikki?"

"Oh, she wasn't sure what time you were going to be back, and Patrick offered to drive her home. The roads are getting bad, and he has that big old sheriff's truck to keep her safe."

"Her safety is important," I murmur, and work to fight off the green-eyed monster rising up from the depths of my stomach. I have nothing to be jealous of, though. Nikki doesn't have a thing for Patrick. If she did, she would have mentioned it to me, right? Seriously though, she can be with any guy she wants. I might not like it and it's not like I've done anything about my feelings for her, and I want her happy... Just not with Patrick.

Or any other guy.

Fuck me.

I don't need to turn to know Brody's eyes are on me. I haven't really opened up about my feelings for Nikki, but he's a smart guy. He clearly knows something is going on, and that I'm a big chicken shit.

"I'm going to head up," Brody says, his voice weary as he gestures toward the stairs.

"Yes, of course," my mom says and kisses her hand and places it on his cheek. He leans into it, a smile on his face. "I'll see you in the morning." She grins. "I hear Santa is close."

"Thanks, Donna." My heart beats hard for my friend. I'm glad I could give him this nice family Christmas, and I really hope he can fix things with Josie. They belong together.

Nikki and I belong together.

"I'm going to head up too," I say to Mom and throw my arms around her for a big hug. "I'll see you in the morning."

"Will you be having breakfast before you go with Nikki to the gravesite?"

My phone buzzes and I tug it from my pocket, hoping it's Nikki. It's not. Disappointment sits in my gut as I shove it back into my pocket. I give Brody a nod as he disappears up the stairs, and frown when I turn back to Mom.

"Did Nikki say anything before she left?" It's not like her to just leave, no text to let me know what was going on. I told her I'd be back as fast as I could, and I'd take her home. Maybe she got tired of waiting.

"No, was she supposed to say something?" she asks, her eyes narrowed like she's searching her brain because she might have forgotten something important.

I shake my head. "No, I'm just a bit surprised and I haven't heard from her. I'm sure she'll text soon, and I'm assuming we won't be heading to the gravesite until after breakfast and presents are open."

She kisses her hands and places them on my cheeks. "It's so nice that you go with her every year."

"She's my best friend. It's what friends do for each other." My heart pinches tight as I think back to the night she lost her mom. We were just kids, only five years old. It was a confusing and sad time for everyone, and Nikki spent most of that first week at my place. I could hear her cry at night, and I'd sneak in to sleep with her and wipe the tears from her face.

"You've been a good friend to her."

Maybe then, but have I lately? I barely speak to her during the NHL season. Thinking about her when I'm away, in a hotel room that looks like every other, or during a game, always fucks me over, and yeah, here I am hating that she might be with someone else, when I'm a well-known man-whore. As awful as it sounds, I bury myself in other women with the hopes of getting one out of my head. It hasn't worked yet, and you know what, I am getting damn tired of it all.

What are you going to do about that, dude?

I pull my phone from my pocket again and run my fingers over the screen. Is it too late to text? I don't want to wake her up, but I can't shake the feeling that something is off between us. In the bathroom, I brush my teeth, and tug my shirt off as I walk back to my bedroom. Downstairs, the front door opens and closes, Aunt Jeannie finally calling it a night. Whispered words reach my ears as Mom and Dad put parcels under the tree. No matter how old I am, Santa still comes to the Bradbury house.

I glance at the little box on my nightstand, my gift to Nikki. We usually exchange gifts on Christmas Eve, which makes her sudden departure all that more confusing. Maybe she's not feeling well? She did have the sniffles the other day.

I strip off and climb between the sheets, and check my phone one more time. I wait one minute, until my clock reads midnight, and I send her a text.

Me: *Merry Christmas.*

I stare at my phone for a long time, and I'm about to set it down when three dots appear. I adjust my pillow and get ready for a texting session. We've been doing that all week, and some of the tension eases inside me. But after a long time, her text comes in, and it's wishful thinking on my part that we slip from texting to sexting, but the two words that appear on my screen send those thoughts running for the hills, and floods my body with unease.

. . .

Nikki: *Merry Christmas.*

I stare at my phone, waiting for more but nothing comes. Chest tight, I try to take a breath, but my lungs are a bit constricted. I struggle to tamp down my worries. I'm sure come tomorrow, when I show up to take her and her dad to the gravesite, all will be good, and I can't forget Christmas isn't always twinkling lights and sugar cookies for everyone. Some people, especially those who've had loss, have a hard time with the holiday.

I drop my phone, and put my arm over my head, willing sleep to come. I drift off, but have strange dreams that pull me awake. This goes on for a few more hours, until first light, and the sound of Brody's footsteps walking down the hall pulls me awake. I guess he's off to try to patch things up with Josie. While I'd like to hightail it to Nikki's, it's too early. I lay there for a couple more hours and when I hear Mom and Dad in the kitchen, trying to be quiet, I rush downstairs, eager to get on with my day...eager to see Nikki.

"Merry Christmas," I say, injecting enthusiasm into my voice when I enter the kitchen and find Mom and Dad cooking up a storm. But those two words, and the simple text from Nikki last night, churn in my stomach. "Coffee," I mumble going right for the pods.

Mom laughs at me. "Not much has changed since you were a child." She hands me the milk. "Still can't sleep when you know Santa is coming."

I laugh. "You know me. I love presents." I glance over Dad's shoulder as he cooks a full package of bacon. "Need any help?" I ask, although I fear I'm not going to be able to choke it down, not when my stomach is in knots.

"Grab the plates," Dad says.

Ten minutes later, we're seated around the table, and Mom frowns. "Should you go get Brody up?"

"Sorry, I should have told you. He left early this morning." I check the time. He's been gone for hours, so I can only hope that's a good sign.

Mom has a little twinkle in her eye when she grins. "They make such a cute couple. It's nice to see all your friends settling down, Declan." She takes a deep breath and lets it out, and while she's not saying anything about my single status, she's saying everything about it.

My phone pings and I snatch it from the table, and smile when I see it's from Brody, letting me know things are good and he'll call me later.

"Was that Nikki?" Mom asks.

"No, Brody." I set my phone down, and find it hard to keep the smile on my face as worry prowls through me.

"Why don't we wait on the presents," Mom says.

I nod. While I hate to rush off, everything in my gut is telling me I need to go, and I need to go now.

NIKKI

C hristmas Day:

Despite the twinkling lights, and the fresh Christmas snow falling on our lawn, my insides are a turbulent mess of loss and sadness. I left the party last night without saying goodbye to Declan, without exchanging gifts like we've done for years. That's so not like me. In fact, I told him I'd wait for him—I always wait for him—but as the night progressed, the strange, urgent need to flee, to save my heart and soul, forced me into action. I'm not sure what came over me, maybe it had something to do with my friend Josie telling me the town's sheriff was interested in me, and deep in my heart I knew I had to move on.

I'm not sure if Patrick sensed the panic in me last night, but when he offered to drive me home in his big, sturdy truck— I'm not a fan of slippery roads—I accepted. He's a nice man, a good man, a man any woman would be lucky to have. The problem for me is that my heart belongs to another. But I can't be with Declan, not just because he'll only ever see me as a friend, but I'm not the right girl for him. I take a deep breath and let it out slowly as I stand at the living room window, taking in the quiet streets, and hug myself as the coffee maker beeps.

"Hey kiddo, coffee's ready," Dad says from the kitchen, and I push off the sill and glance at the twinkling lights reflecting off the picture frame on the mantel—mom in her wedding dress.

I put a smile on my face for my Dad's sake. It's Christmas after all, and despite the losses we've suffered, we honestly have so much to be thankful for. The smell of turkey roasting in the oven reaches my nostrils. Normally Christmas dinner is just the two of us, but tonight Dad invited a friend from work. Apparently, she's new in town, with no family close by, and since Dad's motto is no one eats alone in Holiday Peak, she'll be seated at our table tonight.

"Roads look slippery." I worry my lip between my teeth as Dad hands me a steamy cup of coffee. I take a big sip and moan my approval. "Maybe we should wait until the plows clear the streets before we go to the gravesite."

"Up to you." He scratches his unshaven face. As the manager at the local bank, Dad's a suit and tie kind of guy, but come the holidays, he kicks back and relaxes, which makes me happy. You know what else would make me happy? If he found love again. The man dedicated his life to raising me, trying to be mother and father, and he deserves happiness more than anyone I know. "I'm good either way." He lifts his coffee cup, and glances at me over the rim, his graying brows raised. "Will Declan be joining us?"

I almost laugh. He knows me far too well, and clearly senses something is off and when something is off, it usually has to do with Declan. This Christmas is going to be different from the rest, though. Whenever Declan comes home, I drop everything to spend every minute with him, and when he says goodbye, it always leaves me alone and lonely. I just can't keep doing this to myself. I'm determined to break the pattern once and for all.

"No, I don't think so. He's with his family, and he has a friend staying with them this year." I inject lightness in my tone and add, "We'll go, just you and me." It's been Dad and me for so long, I can't see life any other way. Not that I'm complaining. I love my Dad. He's my rock, and I can't see getting my own place when he has this big house. Or maybe it's the thoughts of leaving a place that holds such strong memories of my mother. I don't remember much. I was only five when we lost her, but what I do remember, I hold close.

He stands, and his ankle cracks. "Florida is looking better and better," he says. "These old bones are done with the cold."

"You'll never leave Holiday Peak," I say with a wave of my hand.

"I think you're wrong. I think it's time for Florida winters."

I just shake my head at him. He's been talking about Florida for years now, but I'm not sure if he's serious. Sometimes I think he wants to move just to get me moving, but onto what?

"Maybe you should come too."

"My life is here, Dad."

He eyes me. "You can work anywhere, kiddo." His face falls, goes a bit serious. "You're not staying here because of me, right?" he asks, and not for the first time. "It's a big world out there, Nikki. Don't miss out on it because you think you need to stay here and take care of me."

I swallow the lump in my throat. There's a part of me that can't argue with him. Maybe it's true, maybe I can't leave Holiday Peak, or this house, because I'd be too worried about him being lonely.

"No Dad, that's not the reason," I say and avert my gaze. "I have nowhere to go, and I love my job here."

"Didn't you always say that you wanted to travel and someday open your own salon?"

"I will, eventually." My phone pings, and I'm grateful for the reprieve, as I pick it up from the counter. Half expecting it to be Declan, my stomach tightens. I need to text him, and tell him he doesn't need to escort me to the gravesite, that Dad and I are going to go alone. *What's stopping you?* Oh, just the fact that it's something we've done for years and it's not that I want to just blow him off, he's my best friend, but I need to put a measure of distance between us once and for all. My heart is on the line here.

Just then the doorbell rings, and my gaze jerks to Dad when he says, "I guess Declan didn't get the memo."

"I...I..." Shit, once I see his handsome face, that adorable smile of his, I'll cave and invite him along. But I'm only getting myself in deeper, and I have to stop this now. He's not into me, and I'm not the girl for him, anyway. Deep in my heart, I know that. He might not be ready to settle down just yet, but when he does, and I suspect it will be soon, he needs a wife who can give him the big family he wants.

He always talked about having enough kids to make his own hockey team. That's far too many kids as far as I'm concerned. As an only child, he wanted siblings, lots of them. But I can't be a mom. I don't know the first thing about it. Sure, I had Dad, but without motherly guidance, I have no idea how to be feminine or nurturing. That's why the boys let me into the treehouse, I guess. Declan saw me as one of the guys back then, and nothing has changed over the years. Even if he did start looking at me differently, I can't give him what he wants. I don't want to mess up any kid's life, and if I'm being honest, there's a part of me that's afraid something will happen to me, and I'll leave my child behind. I know the pain from that and couldn't bear it for another child to go through what I went through.

"Do you want me to get it?" Dad asks, pulling my thoughts back.

"I...no...I'll get it." This is my problem, not Dad's, so I need to stay strong and deal with it. Phone in hand, I glance at the message from a co-worker, and hurry to the other room. I pull open the front door to find a very cold and snowy Patrick standing on the stoop.

"Patrick," I say, and glance around to see what's going on. It can't be a good thing when the sheriff shows up at your door unexpectedly. A shiver goes through me as I recall the last time that happened, and the loss we suffered afterward. It was right before Christmas, on snow-covered roads. His truck lights aren't flashing, but that doesn't mean something bad hasn't happened.

"Is everything...everyone...okay?" I ask, doing my best not to panic. Brody has that ridiculous sports car which isn't fit for winter in Holiday Peak. What if he and Declan...

Patrick takes his hat off, and gives me a reassuring smile. "Perfectly fine. I was doing rounds this morning, and it's pretty slippery out there. I thought you and your father might like an escort to the cemetery. We can take my truck. Those tires will plow through an avalanche."

My heart squeezes tight. He really is such a nice man. I don't feel any kind of spark for him, but maybe I would over time. Maybe I should give him a chance. Maybe he won't want things from me that I can't give.

"You are the sweetest," I say to him and his smile widens. "Come in, come in." I back up and wave my hand. He kicks snow off his boots, and brushes the flakes from his shoulders before he enters.

"Patrick, so nice to see you. Business or pleasure?" Dad asks as he comes from the kitchen. I quickly explain that Patrick wants to drive us and Dad gestures him to join us for a cup of coffee first.

That's when I realize I'm still in my Rudolf pajamas, and must look a mess. I smooth my messy bed hair down, and point to the stairs. "You go ahead and have coffee. I'll get a quick shower and get ready."

"Take your time. Things are quiet this morning."

Dad engages Patrick in conversation as I dart upstairs. I shower quickly, pull on my jeans and a big comfy sweater. Unlike the women Declan is photographed with, this is how I prefer to dress.

Stop thinking about him already.

As I work on that, my gaze goes to the present on my nightstand. Last night's exchange never happened, and I'm not sure I'll see him again this year to give him his gift. I guess things really are changing, and I need to get over the man I can never be with. I glance around my room, which is filled with pictures of Declan and me, from our first birthday party together to last year's Christmas, when he gave me chicken leg socks that go to my mid thighs. I love all the silly gifts he picks up from the states they travel to for hockey. My stomach sours as I reach for my phone and read our last exchange. Before I can give it any more thought, I shoot a text off to Declan.

Me: *Merry Christmas. Dad and I are headed to the cemetery early. Patrick showed up in his truck to drive us, so we're all good. You have a great day with your family and Brody and a safe trip back to Boston. It was great spending time with you, and I'll be watching you win the Stanley Cup!!*

I stare at my words as they blur in front of my watery eyes. Declan is my best friend, and has always been there for me, and in no way do I want to hurt his feelings. But I have to find a way to preserve mine and move forward with life before I find I'm eighty years old and still pining away for my best friend.

I set my phone down and leave it in my room as I head back downstairs. Dad is telling Patrick some old fishing story, and the two are laughing by the time I enter the kitchen.

"Don't believe a word he says," I playfully warn Patrick. "That fish gets bigger and bigger every time he tells that story."

Patrick turns to me, and my breath catches at the way his eyes open, his gaze moving over my face with pure adoration and appreciation. My God, the last time a guy looked at me like that was…never. Okay, well that's not entirely true. Declan looked at me like that last night when he picked me up for the Christmas party. Unlike Patrick though, there wasn't *want* in Declan's eyes and that's for the best in the end anyway.

"You look gorgeous," he says quietly, then color floods his cheeks when Dad clears his throat.

Dad stands. "If you'll excuse me, I'll just grab a sweater."

"I'll get the flowers." I walk into the living room. Patrick follows me in, and I scoop up the basket of plastic flowers for Mom's headstone.

"Pretty," he says, and I turn to find him smiling at me.

"Mom's favorites. Mine too," I admit. "Can't get fresh daisies in the winter, so fake ones have to do."

"That's so nice, Nikki. I know your mom is smiling down on you right now."

My heart skips a couple of beats. "I'll just grab my coat."

We walk to the closet, and I set the basket of flowers down on the table next to the bowl with our keys. Patrick shifts restlessly beside me and it's clear he has something to say.

"Can I ask you something?" he finally blurts out.

"Of course."

"You and Declan, are you—"

"Friends," I say quickly. "We've been good friends since our first day of kindergarten."

And I've been in love with him ever since.

He smooths his hand over his jacket. "I was wondering if maybe you'd like to go out to dinner day after tomorrow? I'm thinking Italian. We'll probably be all in a tryptophan-induced coma with all the turkey leftover after Christmas."

I laugh at that. "You're right, and I think that would be lovely, Patrick. Italian is my favorite."

He shifts from one foot to the other, and his nervousness is rather endearing. "Yeah, I kind of asked your dad. I hope you don't mind."

"Not at all."

I tug my coat from the hanger, and he takes it from me. "Here," he says, and holds it out for me to slip on. I let him help me into my coat, and his hand brushes my arm. I wait for the little shocks of electricity to go through me, the way they go through me when Declan touches me, but they never come.

"Thanks." I pick the flowers up from the table.

"Are you going to the New Year's Eve bash?" he asks as he puts his hat back on, looking so handsome. I just wish he was my type. But no, I gravitate toward one bad boy hockey player with far too many notches in his bedpost.

But he's so much more than that, Nikki.

While that is all true, I need to get him out of my brain, and focus on the man who wants to take me on a date.

"I never miss it," I say. "How about you?"

"I'll be there," he says. "Are you...uh, planning on kissing anyone at midnight?"

"No plans," I tell him, and his smile widens.

The front door flings open, and I nearly jump into Patrick's arms. "Declan," I say, shocked to see him standing there, his body rigid, the muscles in his jaw tight enough to snap. "Did you get my message?"

"I got it."

"Then what…"

"I was already on my way."

I try for light. "As you can see, Patrick is here. He has that big sturdy truck."

I try to tear my gaze away as something that looks like hurt registers in Declan's eyes. "I thought we always…" he waves his hand back and forth between the two of us.

"It's different this year, Declan." I put on my best smile, an add, "You have company you need to be with."

"I need to be with—"

"Declan," Dad says coming around the corner, and there's a part of me that wishes Declan would have finished that sentence, wishes he was going to say, 'I need to be with you.' But that's not going to happen and like I said, I'm not the girl for him. "Merry Christmas, son."

"Hey Declan." Patrick gestures with a nod. "I'll uh, go get the truck started and warmed," he says.

I smile at him. "I'll be right out."

Dad walks past us, and heads outside with Patrick.

Declan frowns, and his gaze goes from me, to Patrick, back to me. "You and…Patrick?"

"He asked me on a date."

I don't know why I'm telling him. It's not like I want to make him jealous. Or maybe it is. God, I'm a mess.

He shoves something small and square into his pocket. "I...I didn't know."

"There's a lot you don't know, Declan," I say, in a low voice. "You're not around much. Maybe you don't even know me anymore."

He glances down, his shoulders rigid. "You're going then... you're going on a date."

My heart squeezes so tight, wanting to pull him in and keep him with me for the rest of my life. But I can't do that, so I ask, "Is there any reason I shouldn't?"

DECLAN

I want to hit something. No, that's putting it too mildly. I want to smash the hell out of something and destroy it. Completely. I take a deep breath to keep myself in check. At times like this, I'd harness this energy and use it in the rink. But I'm not on the road with the team. I'm home and it's Christmas, and my life has just been turned upside down.

What the hell does she mean there's a lot I don't know? That I don't even know her anymore. I call bullshit, because up until ten minutes ago, I thought we knew everything there was to know about each other.

"I can't believe she said that." I talk to myself as I pound on the steering wheel, and drive aimlessly through the quiet streets, not ready to go home just yet, not ready to plaster on a smile and pretend my heart isn't breaking wide open in my chest. But it's my own fault. I never told her how I felt, and I guess there was a small stupid part of me counting on the gift in my pocket to speak for me, since I can't seem to get the words out myself.

When it comes right down to it, there's no reason she shouldn't be with Patrick—other than I hate the idea of it, and it's not Patrick in particular. He's a nice guy. But no guy is good enough for her, myself included, and while I wanted to open my mouth and tell her all the reasons she shouldn't go on that date, I fell silent. She's a gorgeous woman, full of love, life and kindness and honestly, I can't believe she's still single.

Goddamn chicken shit.

I guide the car through the snowy streets as anger builds up inside me. Going to the gravesite every Christmas wasn't just about me driving because she doesn't like snowy roads. It was about being together, being there for her and her dad, taking time out of a busy week to spend some time remembering her mother. Those moments are special to me, meaningful.

Nikki is special, meaningful.

My throat tightens. Oh, shit. Maybe she figured it out. The jewelry box currently in my pocket was on my nightstand last night. Maybe Nikki opened the box, and maybe it scared her off. Christ, I was planning on waiting for her reaction when she opened it, thinking things could go one of two ways. She'd put the ring I had specially made for her on her finger, and realize what it meant. Or she'd laugh, thinking it was just another one of my silly gifts. I guess this morning's dismissive text, and her upcoming date with Patrick has given me the answer I've been looking for. We're to remain in the friend zone, and now I might have even screwed that up.

Shit, shit, shit.

But the truth is, I know her. I know everything about her. Her fears, her dreams, and the only thing I never knew was if she loved me or not. I guess it's not. With my heart heavy, and my throat so tight it hurts to swallow, I slow my car down as the snow grows heavier. My phone buzzes and I pull over to read a text from Brody.

Brody: *Hey bud, sorry again for leaving so early. I'll be staying at Josie's. Things are good.*

My heart pinches, so happy for my friend. He's a good guy and those two belong together. I'm about to text back when another comes in.

Brody: *Are you with Nikki this morning?*

Shit. I don't want to say anything to upset him, not when he's so happy but the truth is, he's my best bud, and I kind of need him right now.

Me: *No, I'm just out for a drive.*

I stare at the phone as three dots appear... my throat tight as I think about Nikki going on a date with Patrick. I should have done something about my feelings for her long before now. I should have told her.

Brody: *Coffee's on. Come over.*

Me: *No, I'm not interrupting.*

Brody: *Get over here right now, or I'm coming to find you.*

Me: *Fine.*

Truthfully, it's what I want. I just don't want to be homing in on their time together. We leave for Boston soon and their relationship is new. The last thing they need is me crying on their shoulder, yet that's just what I'm going to do. Wow, I am seriously pathetic, but I need advice, and maybe the best place to get it is from another woman. I maneuver the quiet streets and spot Brody's car on Main Street. I pull up behind it and kill the ignition. I hurry to the door and I'm about to knock, but Brody is standing there waiting for me. He swings it open, takes one look at me and shakes his head.

"You look like hell."

"Why don't you tell me what you really think."

We head up the stairs and the cold wind follows us up. "I will, as soon as you tell me what you did to screw things up."

"Okay, fair enough."

We enter the loft, and Josie's chocolate lab, Miss Mabel, comes running over to check me out. I drop to my knees. "Sorry girl, no bear claws today." I raise my head when a new set of footsteps sound on the kitchen floor, and I find Josie smiling at me, a mixture of pleasure and concern on her pretty face.

"Coffee?" she asks, but before I can answer, she's already pouring me one. Yeah, I get it. I look like death warmed over.

She hands me the cup and I take a big drink. "Thanks Josie, and Merry Christmas."

"For some, maybe not for others," Brody says and pulls Josie into his arms. She smiles up at him, and places her hand on his chest, and I swear I've never seen a happier couple.

"Come on, let's sit," Josie says.

I nod and let them lead me into the living room, and have to squeeze around a ginormous tree to get a seat at the end of the room. They both drop down onto the sofa, their bodies tight, as Mabel comes my way and sits at my feet, like she's trying to console me. I pat her head, and we all go quiet for a moment as we take in the twinkling lights on the tree.

I finally break the quiet. "She's going on a date with Patrick." Josie makes a small noise and my gaze flies to hers. "What?"

Her cheeks are a bit pale when she says. "I think this is my fault."

"How is it your fault?"

She cringes and snuggles in closer to Brody. "I'm sorry, Declan. She told me you were friends, and Patrick told me he liked her, and he's a nice man, and I suggested maybe she give him a chance, and I thought you were friends..." She stops to take a fast breath. "I should have known better. I'm sorry, Declan. This is my fault."

"It's not your fault. It's my fault."

"How is it your fault?" Brody asks.

"Because I never fucking told her how I felt." I glance at Josie. "Sorry for the language." I sit forward, and brace my elbows on my knees. "This is so messed up. I just never wanted to lose her, you know? Now...I did."

Brody leans closer to me, his eyes heavy with worry. "Tell me exactly what happened."

I recite our morning conversation, and they both sit quietly and listen. We fall silent once I'm done, and Josie eventually breaks it. "She loves you, Declan."

My head lifts. "She's going on a date with Patrick."

"Okay, but can you blame her?"

I sit up a little straighter, going on the defense. "What's that supposed to mean?"

"I don't know you well, and I hope you don't mind me being blunt, but I think she's tired of waiting."

"You think she's been waiting for me?" I shake my head. Is it true? Has she been waiting for me to make the first move? There's a part of me that thinks she could be right, but there's another part that knows Nikki, her fears, and what holds her back in life.

"Last night.... when we got back home, Mom said Nikki left with Patrick because she was tired of waiting."

"Maybe that was your mother's subtle way of telling you what I'm telling you. Nikki doesn't have feelings for Patrick, but she clearly needs to move on because she doesn't see things working out with you two. She loves you, Declan. You love her too. I saw the way you both looked at each other, and no one can question the feelings you two have for one another." She links her fingers together, a nervousness about her, but none of this is her fault. "The way you were together. I guess in the end I chalked it up to close friendship, but I was wrong."

"Okay, so now we need to fix it," Brody says, and he takes Josie's twisted fingers in his hands and smooths out her worries. "Isn't that what you said to me last night when I thought I fucked everything up between Josie and me?"

"Yeah." My voice is low, absent, as I continually run over this morning's conversation. "She told me I didn't know who she was."

"There you go," Josie says.

I lift my head, but her words aren't registering. "What do you mean?"

"Do you know her?" she asks.

"Yeah, better than anyone in the world," I say quietly and instantly question myself. I never would have questioned it in the past, but things are different this year. Maybe Nikki is right. Maybe a lot has changed since I've been home last, and I don't know her anymore.

No!

My brain instantly does a one-eighty before that thought settles. It's bullshit. My brain knows it and so does my heart.

"Then show her how much you know her. Prove her wrong."

An invisible band tightens around my chest, making breathing difficult. "I know what she likes, what she wants and what she's afraid of. Just like she knows me. We tell each other things we've never told anyone else, and sometimes we don't even have to tell the other person. We just know."

"Declan, why do you think she's still single then? She's a beautiful woman, bright and funny and yet she's still single, spending all her time with you when you get home. You can't expect her to wait forever."

"She's been waiting...do you really think?"

Josie's smile is full of warmth and compassion when she says, "It's time you found out what *she* thinks, and for you to tell her what *you* think."

"If you know her like you say you do, this should be easy, bro."

I take a breath, and consider everything. I'm in love with my best friend, and she's going on a date with another guy, and if Josie is right, it's because she's tired of waiting around for me. Christ, I need to act and act fast. But there's more to it than that—so much more to Nikki—so many things that frighten her and create roadblocks to her happiness, which, now that I think about it, is probably why I'm so confused, one minute thinking she wants something with me, and the next thinking she can't.

"No, you're wrong, Brody. It's not going to be easy. It's going to be hard."

"When have you ever been afraid of hard?"

"When it comes to Nikki. I love her and I can't lose her."

"Then we fight."

"I'm going to have to call Coach. I can't go back before New Year's." My mind races, putting a plan together. Shit, I have one week to pull off what's going through my brain, but with the holiday and very few businesses open, I'm going to have to call in some big-ass favors.

"I'll stay and help."

"Thanks, because it's going to take the whole town to help me pull off what I have in mind."

I just hope I'm not too late.

NIKKI

F ive Days until New Year's Eve:

I stand at the window and take two very deep breaths as I check my phone for the millionth time, struggling to convince myself that letting Declan go is for the best. He's my best friend no matter what, so I shot him off a text last night wishing him safe travels home and a successful hockey season. He responded with a 'thanks' and that he'll see me soon. I'm not sure what he meant by that. He's gone now for the rest of the season. His present is still sitting on my dresser and whatever he had for me, I guess it's to remain unknown.

Dad comes into the room, and I turn to find him looking handsome in his dress pants and shirt. It's the holidays and he loves to kick back, but at dinner the other night with his friend Carol, who was so lovely, I did notice that he was clean shaven and I'm pretty sure I got a whiff of the cologne I got him for Christmas. Honestly, I was expecting someone my age, not a woman in her mid-fifties. I'm not sure why. Perhaps I thought she was starting her career at the bank here, not finishing it.

"Don't you look nice," I say, and smile.

He grins. "You're one to talk."

I laugh and glance down at the dress. "This old thing. It's been hanging in my closet for years." It's not a lie. I don't wear dresses often, mostly just once a year when I go to Declan's parents' Christmas Eve party. "But this isn't about me. Where are you going looking so handsome?"

"I thought I'd show Carol around. Maybe take her out for a bite to eat."

My heart pinches. "That's so nice," I say, playing it cool, yet hoping this is the beginning of something special for him. "I really like her."

"Do you?" he asks eagerly, then as he chills himself out, and I try not to smirk, he clears his throat and says, "She likes you too." I don't dare ask if I'm going to be getting a stepmother, but secretly hoping I am. "She's from Boston. Transferred from there." He laughs. "Next stop, Florida."

Before I can respond, the doorbell rings, and I spin. "That's probably Patrick."

"Declan's gone?" he asks.

I avoid his gaze. I don't want him to see the sadness on my face. "Yes," I say lightly. "He and Brody went back today."

"That's odd."

"What's odd about that?" I ask, and I walk to the door.

"I was sure I saw them both in town earlier when I was out for a walk."

"Maybe they had some last-minute things to do." I swallow and reach for the door handle, hoping I don't run into him if he hasn't left yet. I might do something foolish, like tell him how I feel. That would be a stupid mistake, and maybe accepting this date with Patrick was too. I guess by the end of the night, I'll know him better, and I'll know if we're compatible.

Compatible?

That's what you want, Nikki?

Where's the passion, the want, the need to tear clothes off because you just can't get enough of one another?

I plaster on a smile and swing the door open to find a very handsome Patrick standing on the stoop, flowers in his hands. God, he looks so nervous. "For me?" I ask.

He holds out the bouquet. "For you."

I take them from him and smell the pretty roses. "Come in. Just let me put these in water."

Dad picks up the conversation with Patrick as I fill a vase with water and arrange the flowers, all the while ignoring the knot in my stomach. Everything inside me knows this isn't right, and while I don't want to lead Patrick on—he's such a nice man—I'm not sure I can develop feelings for him.

Give it a chance, girl.

I step back into the room and the second I do, Patrick glances at me, warm appreciation in his eyes, and that's when it occurs to me. Patrick likes me. I like Patrick. He's lonely. I'm lonely. But there's no spark between us. It's not there when he looks at me, and it's not there when I look at him. I think we both know it. My stomach settles. We're going to be friends and we're going to enjoy a nice dinner together.

"I'm ready."

"You look beautiful, Nikki."

"Thank you." I reach into the closet for my coat.

"Better grab a hat and scarf. It's bitter cold. I kept the truck running so you'd be warm when you got in."

"Very thoughtful."

He holds my coat out and I slide into it, then I put on a hat, scarf and mitts. Not really an attractive look, but that's okay.

"You two have a nice night," Dad calls out.

"You too, Dad," I say and the cold air falls over us, turning my breath to fog as we step outside. Patrick puts his arm around me to keep me from falling on my ass in my boots, as he guides me to the passenger side of the truck.

Once inside, I remove my mitts and glance at him, taking in his features through the dashboard light. He backs out of my driveway and instead of heading into town, he goes the opposite direction.

I glance around. I'm not much into surprises. Okay, well maybe that's not entirely true. When we were kids, Declan always surprised me with adventures, and I loved it.

"Where are we going?"

"I thought we'd get out of town, head to Malden. They have a really great Italian restaurant there."

"Oh, I haven't been there in ages. Sounds fun."

As we drive the snowy roads, he turns on his wipers and the window blurs. A car passes us on the other side of the street, and my heart jumps. Was that...Brody's car? Why would he still be in town? Maybe he decided to stay longer to be with Josie. Is Declan still here too? He would have told me that when he texted me back, right? Or not. Under the circumstances, I haven't been the best of friends with him. He seemed so shocked that I accepted a date with Patrick. I guess I can't blame him. I don't usually date, and I do drop everything to be with Declan over the holidays. Could he have been jealous? Nah, that's just crazy thinking. He's traveling the country, breaking hearts. They don't call him the Heart Breaker for nothing, and I'd be wise, moving forward, to better protect mine.

We drive by town hall, and I note all the cars in the lot, and all the lights on inside. "Are they decorating for New Year's already?"

"I guess they're getting an early start on things."

"No one called me to let me know they were starting early. I always help out. I thought we were all gathering in two days. They'll probably be done by then if they're already at it."

He smiles at me and pulls onto the highway ramp. The snow picks up again, and worry careens through my blood. "Maybe we shouldn't be on the highway."

He casts me a glance as I worry my fingers, playing with the strap of my purse. "If you're not comfortable, we can turn back, but this thing handles well in the snow."

I'm about to ask if we can turn back, when a scream crawls out of my throat. I grip the dashboard to brace myself, as Patrick turns his attention back to the road, as an oncoming car swerves into our lane, and misses us by inches as it nose-dives into the ditch.

Patrick carefully slows the vehicle down, and pulls to the side of the road. I reach for the door, and he stops me. "You better wait here. Let me check it out," he says, going into sheriff mode. I nod, my insides a total mess as I throw up a prayer that whoever just went off the road is okay.

I sit still, my body ice cold as Patrick calls in the accident and exits the vehicle. I hold my breath as he disappears into the ditch. I grab my phone, and Declan is the person I usually text when I'm upset, but I can't do that. Not anymore. I rock in my seat, anxious for Patrick to reappear, and when he finally does, he has a woman in his arms.

A cry of sorts crawls out of my throat, as I quickly jump from the vehicle so he can set her inside. He comes up to me, worry on his face, as the sound of sirens reach my ears. The woman in his arms makes a sound and I take a breath of relief that she's conscious.

"Are you okay?" I ask her, and put her in her early forties, around Patrick's age.

"I...I am. Just shaken up." She beams up at Patrick. "Thank you for stopping."

"I'm the sheriff," he says.

Her eyes go wide. "You're Patrick?"

He nods. "You know me?"

"I'm on my way to my sister's in Holiday Peak. Veronica Miller."

"Of course. Veronica did say her sister was visiting. She invited me for dinner tomorrow night as a matter of fact." He frowns. "She told you about me?"

I can't see it in the dark, but I'm pretty sure the woman is blushing and that's when it occurs to me that Veronica had plans to set her sister up with the sheriff. I bite back a grin.

"Oh, yes. She told me about everyone in the town. I didn't think we'd meet this way."

An ambulance pulls over behind our vehicle. "You'll have to go to the hospital. Just to be sure, okay?"

"I don't like ambulances." She clings to the sheriff, and he glances at me, and it's easy to tell he's struggling to do the right thing.

"Why don't you go with her?" I suggest. "I can drive your truck back."

"Like hell you will." I spin at the sound of Declan's voice, and as he comes toward me, all power and muscles and determination, I nearly drop to the ground. He puts his arms around me and tugs me to him. His gaze moves over my face in a careful assessment as I go weak in the knees and cling to him. "Are you okay?"

"I think she might be faint from the shock of the accident," Patrick explains.

"What are you...doing here?" I ask, my voice low and breathless.

He goes quiet for a second, like he's trying to come up with a reason, and when he says, "Just got a late start, and I uh...was talking to Jon," he gestures with a nod to the paramedic.

"When the call came in," I know he's lying to me, or at least telling partial truths. What is going on? What is he hiding?

"But, you knew I was here?"

"When I called it in, I said you were in the truck with me."

I shake my head. I guess I was so worked up about the car crossing the road in front of us, I didn't hear that.

"I'll take her home," Declan says. "I can drive you back to get your truck later."

"That's okay, I'll get one of my men to get it."

I let Declan hold me as they load the woman onto the stretcher and put her in the ambulance.

"Thank God, she's okay," I say, my body shivering from the adrenaline dump.

"You're not, so come on. I want to get you home and into bed."

I swallow, wishing he wasn't putting me to bed as a friend, but something more.

Stop.

"No, I don't want to take you from whatever you were doing."

Completely ignoring me, he leads me to his dad's car, which he's borrowed during his time home, and carefully sets me in the passenger seat. God, it feels so good to be held by him, but if he's busy.

"Declan—"

"I'm taking you home, end of story."

"I don't remember you being so stubborn," I huff out, even though I'm so happy to be here beside him.

"Yeah, well maybe there are things you don't know about me either, Nikki," he says. I sit there and stare at him. What the hell does he mean by that? I know everything about him. But right now, with my body worked up and shaking, I close my mouth and let him take me home. The place is dark by the time we get there, and I'm glad Dad has gone out with Carol.

"Thanks," I say and unbuckle, but before I can get out of the car, Declan is right there, opening my door, and lifting me out. He scoops me up, carries me to the stairs and asks me for my key. I fish it from my purse and hand it over. A few minutes later, he's setting me on my bed and tugging off my boots. My heart wobbles. I guess he really knows what seeing that vehicle go off the road has done to me.

He stands up, tugs off his clothes, and while I've seen his body numerous times, it never fails to impress me.

"What are you doing?"

He doesn't answer, instead he walks to my dresser, opens the drawer and grabs me a nightie. "Get changed."

"I..." He turns, keeping his back to me to give me privacy. "What's going on?"

"I'm staying. You have two minutes to change, or I'm doing it for you. Then I want you to crawl into that bed, and make room for me."

With my brain on hyperdrive, I quickly scramble out of my coat and dress, and tug on my nightie. I slide between the sheets, and curl up on one side. I pinch my eyes shut, and my body goes cold again, as that car going off the road flashes in my mind's eye.

His feet sound on the floor, and the bed dips beside me as he slides in. Two seconds later, I'm the little spoon to his big spoon, and he puts his arm around me to pull me close, and warm me. My heart pounds a little faster. This is exactly how we slept the night my mom died. Declan's parents brought me to their place, and tucked me into a spare room, and as the house settled, the bed dipped beside me and five-year-old Declan hugged me to sleep as I cried.

My throat grows tight as tears pound behind my eyes. He's not even supposed to be here tonight, yet here he is, his strong body wrapped around mine to keep me warm and safe. My God, he is so sweet and sensitive to my needs and...the love I had for him then only grew stronger over the years. I am in so much trouble here.

DECLAN

F our Days until New Year's Eve:

The early morning sun slants on the wall and pulls me awake. I inch back and glance at Nikki as she sleeps soundly beside me. Every muscle in my body tenses as my mind goes back to last night, to what could have happened on those snow-covered roads.

Jesus, a bunch of us were all at the town hall, putting my plans into motion, when Patrick called in the accident. I was standing beside Jon when he got the call, and what happened after that can only be described as an adrenaline-infused blur. I can only remember going on auto-pilot, the need to get to Nikki, and ensure she was safe, driving my actions.

I take a couple deep breaths, and shake my head. If anything had happened to her... Nope, can't go there. She's safe, and I'm glad I was able to get her home and give her comfort. I slide from the bed, taking care not to wake her, and tug on my clothes. The door creaks when I open it and I glance back, to make sure she's still asleep. I tip toe downstairs and head to the kitchen to put on a pot of coffee.

Footsteps sound behind me and I turn to find Nikki's dad Tom coming to an abrupt stop when he sees me at the counter, my hair a mess, like I'd just crawled out of bed—his daughter's bed—which of course, I did. But it's the movement behind him that catches my attention. I bite back a grin, when I realize what's going on, but Tom doesn't need to worry. No one here is doing the walk of shame this morning, and I'm glad to see him with someone.

"Declan," he says and glances over his shoulder, his body tense, nervous. "I saw your car last night when we…uh, I got home. I didn't realize you stayed over." A pretty woman comes up behind him, and I smile at her. Tom shifts. "Declan, this is Carol. Carol this is—"

"Declan Bradbury," she says and crosses the room to shake my hand. "It's so nice to meet you. What a lovely surprise."

Tom frowns. "Is everything okay?"

"Everything is fine."

"Last I knew, Nikki was going on a date with Patrick."

"There was an accident." Tom's face pales, and he reaches for the kitchen chair. "Nikki's fine, she's sleeping," I say quickly. Jesus, I should have opened with that. "I do need to talk to you about something."

"Of course." He sits, and I pour three mugs of coffee.

I drop down in the seat across from him, and figure out how to start this conversation. "Do you think Nikki is into Patrick?"

A knowing grin crosses his face. "Declan, she's into you. Surely you know that." I stare at him, and he laughs. "You two have been in love with each other for as long as I can remember. The only two people in the world who don't know it are you and Nikki."

"You think she loves me?" Josie said the same thing. So did my buddy Brody, but I think I still need more convincing, because man, I have a plan in motion, and I don't want to fuck up anything between us.

Things are already fucked up, dude.

Yeah, that's right. She was on a date with Patrick last night. "She said I didn't know her."

He angles his head, confused. "Why would she say that?"

"I do know her."

"Tell her you do."

I scrub my chin, my mind racing. "No, I can't just tell her. That's not enough. I want to show her." I lean in, and lower my voice. "I want to show her how much I know her and how much I love her."

A wide smile splits his lips. "What do you have in mind?"

I keep my voice low as I tell him my plan, and he sits there grinning, and that makes me happy. Nikki worries about her father, worries about leaving him alone, but now that he has someone, maybe that will change things for her.

"What's going on?"

I lift my head and both Tom and Carol turn at the sound of Nikki's voice. "Did we wake you, kiddo?" Tom asks.

"No." Her glance flits to me, nervous, unsure.

Her father stands and hugs her. "Declan told us about the accident. Are you okay?"

Her gaze goes from her father to Carol, back to her father. "I am, but I'm going to head over to the hospital. I got a text from Patrick. It was Veronica Miller's sister, Violet, who was in the accident." She holds her phone up and my heart stalls. Jesus, I hope she's not falling for him, and he's not falling for her. I try to tamp down the measure of panic, ready to take myself outside and kick my own ass for being a chicken shit all these years. We belong together and I'm damn well going to prove it.

Nikki smiles at her father's friend. "Nice to see you again, Carol."

"It was late when we got back and the roads—"

Nikki puts her hand up to stop her dad. "It's okay, Dad. No explanation needed." My heart swells with the way she looks at her dad. There's so much love there, and it makes her happy to see him happy. She's been doing things for others her whole life, and dammit I want to be taking care of her.

"I'll drive you to the hospital," I say. I actually have to talk to Patrick, but I don't tell her that.

"It's okay—"

"The roads aren't great, Nikki. Let Declan drive you," her father says.

She hesitates for a second, and plucks at her nightie, which falls over her curves so nicely. "I'm sure you must have to get back to Boston by now."

"Boston can wait." I stand, and set my mug in the sink. "Do you want to get coffee and breakfast on the way, or afterward?" I ask, partly because she's probably starving, and partly because I'd like to give Tom and Carol some privacy this morning. Nikki nods, no doubt thinking the same thing as I am about her Dad.

"Just give me a minute to change. I want to get there right away, so we'll get breakfast afterward and I'll shower when I get back."

"Do I still have a toothbrush here?" I ask, with a grin. It's not the first time I've stayed over, but it's the first time I've stayed in Nikki's bed in a long time. I gave that up when I got my first boner lying next to her.

"I think I can find you a new one," Nikki says with a chuckle and I follow her up the stairs. She stops outside the bathroom door. "Second drawer on the left."

I head into the bathroom, and run the toothbrush over my teeth. That's when I realize I left my cell phone on her nightstand. Fuck, I hope she doesn't look at it, or see any of the messages I've been sending. I rinse my mouth and dash into her room, without knocking, and when I do, and find her standing there completely naked...instant boner.

"Fuck," I murmur under my breath as I take in her soft pink nipples, that my mouth wants to explore. My gaze drops to admire the curve of her hips, the soft swell of her tummy, and the trimmed hair between her legs. My legs go weak, the need to pull her to me and kiss every inch of her body smacks me in the face like a high stick. Honest to God, I've seen plenty of naked women before, but none of them can compare to the gorgeous woman before me.

"Declan," she cries out as I continue to stand there, admiring her gorgeous body as she reaches for her shirt to hold it in front of herself.

Her voice kicks my brain back into gear. "Sorry, I should have knocked." I turn, and back into the room.

"What are you doing?"

"My phone. Have to get my phone."

"I can get it for you."

"Nope, that's okay." I snatch it off the nightstand, and it takes every ounce of willpower I have not to turn back around and admire the view. "I'm leaving."

I hurry to the hall, shut her door behind me, and lean against it. Bending forward, I brace my hands on my thighs and work to get myself under control before I run back in there and toss her onto her bed and take her six ways to Sunday. But I can't do that. No, when it comes to Nikki, I need to do right by her, and follow my plan.

I stand upright, and hurry down the stairs. I hover in the living room, wanting to give Tom and Carol privacy. Besides, I have a bunch of messages to answer. I scroll through my phone, hoping my buddy Kane comes through. The guys all know what I'm up to and a few of them, along with their wives and children, are on their way here now, about to invade my parents' home, but Mom and Dad are thrilled, anxious to help me any way they can.

Nikki finally comes down the stairs, and I shove my phone away. She gives me an odd look.

"If I'm keeping you from something, or someone—"

"You're not. Thanks." I pull on my coat and step into my boots.

"See you later, Dad," Nikki calls out when I open the door and gesture for her to go ahead of me, partly because I'm a gentleman, but mostly because I want to see her ass when she walks to my car.

We reach my car and we both climb in. I grin at her as I start the vehicle. "So, your dad and Carol, huh?"

She laughs and it breaks some of the tension between us. "I'm so happy for him."

"Is he still talking about moving to Florida?"

Her smile falls. "Yes."

"Do you think he'll finally do it?"

"I don't know. He thinks the reason I'm still here is because I worry about him."

I nod and back the car out. When I get us on the main street, I ask, "Are you?"

She swallows. "I just...I don't want to leave him alone."

"Maybe he's talking about moving, to get you moving."

"Yeah," she says under her breath.

"You used to talk about traveling the world. You don't talk about that anymore."

She nods, goes quiet for a moment and then says, "Dad said the same thing to me."

"Maybe he figures if he's not here anymore, you'll go live the life you were meant to live."

"I am living life," she says, but we both know she's not. Not really. Hockey is my dream job, but it's not my life. No, the life I want is with Nikki.

"What about Tuscany?"

Her nose crinkles. "What about it?"

"I mean, that's the first place on your bucket list, isn't it?"

"I don't think I ever told you that."

"Yeah, well there's a reason you watched Under the Tuscan Sun four billion times."

"Four billion? I told you a million times to stop exaggerating."

We both laugh at that, then she goes serious. "You used to tell me about all the places you went on vacation when you were younger, and how you couldn't wait until we got older so we could go together. You don't talk about that anymore either."

My stomach tightens. "I know."

"But I get it," she says, throwing a smile my way. "Your life is crazy busy."

She's right. It is. But I never should have let it overtake everything, including Nikki. I have a lot to make up for and I'm not letting fear hold me back any longer.

"If your father finally went south, would you start living your dreams?"

"It's a little too late for that now, don't you think?"

"I don't think it's too late for anything. You heard about that eighty-two-year-old female astronaut going into space, right?"

She laughs. "I want to explore the world, not space."

I take a turn and ease my vehicle into a parking spot near the hospital. "Thanks for driving me. I'm anxious to talk to Violet."

"And Patrick?" I ask, working to keep my voice even.

Her gaze flies to mine. "You sound like you're jealous."

I shrug, and since I want this woman in my life more than I want my next breath, it's time to start dropping the hints. "Maybe I am." She goes perfectly still, and I stop breathing as I wait for her response. When one doesn't come, I ask, "What?"

"I'm sure any one of your bunnies on the road will console you," she says a teasing look in her eyes, but beneath it there's pain. Is that pain because she wants to be with me?

"Maybe it's not the bunnies I want, Nikki," I say, boldly.

She frowns and glances down, and I wish I could hear whatever it is going through her brain, but maybe I already know, and maybe it's a good thing my friends are bringing their families.

"Typical guy," she jokes.

"What's that supposed to mean?"

"Nothing, and I mean it in the most loving way, best friend." She opens her door. "I'll be back in a few minutes." I open my door and follow her out. I need to have a conversation with Patrick. "You don't have to come."

"Yeah, I do. What if you collapse again?"

"Patrick will be there," she explains, and jealousy rips through me again. "If I collapse, he's trained."

"You're mine, not his," I grumble under my breath, every ounce of possessiveness I have toward Nikki clamoring to the surface.

"What?"

"I said you're my best friend, not his."

She nods, and gives up the fight when I start walking with her. Inside, we check in at the nursing station and take the elevator to Violet's room. We step inside and find Patrick sitting on a chair next to the bed.

"Patrick," Nikki says and his head lifts. Warmth fills his eyes, warmth for a friend, not a lover, and I gauge Nikki's reaction to the sheriff. There's no spark, no chemistry. My racing heart settles, because Josie was right about their relationship. So why did Nikki agree to go out with him if there was nothing between them?

She's tired of waiting for you.

And what are you doing about that, dude?

Oh, just everything, and I pray to God it's enough.

NIKKI

Three Days Until New Year's Eve:

I'm supposed to be on days off from Chatters, the hair salon where I work, but I got called in first thing this morning, with a full client load—none of my regulars, which is odd. I'm shocked, to be honest. We're usually busy before Christmas and maybe Christmas Eve for those wanting a cut for the big Holiday Peak party at town hall. Yesterday, after seeing Patrick—I think he's found his match with Violet—I guess we won't be sharing that New Year's kiss like he alluded to, and I think that's for the best. Although today I was supposed to help out with the decorating at the hall, and now I can't since I'm swamped. I was also looking forward to spending time with Dad, but he's been busy with Carol, and while I'm happy for him, I'm feeling a little sad...a little lonely.

I step into Coffee Klatch, and wave to Mabel—Josie named her dog Miss Mabel, after the lovely woman behind the counter—as she pours coffee from behind the counter. I breathe in the fresh smell, in desperate need for a cup. I haven't seen Declan since he dropped me off at home yesterday after we checked in on Violet. She had a mild concussion, and Patrick very quickly offered to watch over her. Declan said goodbye at my door, yet I keep catching glimpses of him. At least I think it's him. He must be gone back to Boston by now, right?

"Mocha latte, and a cinnamon roll," Mabel says, and I grin as she slides my order across the counter. She glances at my clothes. I always wear a black shirt and pants to work, and my most comfy shoes. No need to get dressed up when I wear a big heavy apron. "Are you on your way to work?"

"Yes, I suddenly have a full day." I take a sip of my coffee. "I didn't think there was a full moon tonight," I tease.

"Weird things do happen during the full moon," she assures me, a tiny spark in her eyes. "But sometimes weird things happen without a full moon, too. Sometimes great things happen when we have Christmas snow."

I glance over my shoulder and fresh new flakes begin to fall. I didn't think snow was forecast for today, but like my favorite meteorologist, who lives a couple doors down, always says to me: the only thing we can count on is light today, dark tonight. I grin and ask, "Ah, what is Christmas snow?"

"It's the snow that falls between Christmas and the New Year. It's magical." She says it so nonchalantly, I can't tell if she's kidding or not.

"Have you been watching too many Hallmark movies?" I chuckle, but it holds no humor because honestly, at this point, I'm pretty sure happily ever after only exists in fantasy.

"Oh honey, you're too young to be this jaded. Christmas snow is magic. You'll see."

Okay, not kidding.

She leans across the counter. "Have you heard about the new romance blossoming?" My heart jumps for a bit. Is she talking about Declan? He's been hanging around town for some reason, and I'm suspecting he's found himself a Christmas fling. Declan doesn't do long term. Before I can answer, she says, "Patrick and Violet. Veronica had plans to set them up this year."

I tuck my cinnamon roll into my big purse. "You knew about that?"

"Yeah, I knew about your date with him too." She waves her hand at me. "But he's not the guy for you."

I take a deep breath and let it out slowly. "Don't think there is a guy out there for me." That's a lie, Declan is the guy for me, but...so many reasons we can't be together.

"Believe in that Christmas snow," she says as the door jingles and in walks another customer. I sip my coffee and break off bites of my cinnamon roll as I walk to Chatters.

With Christmas snow on my mind, I think back to my conversation with Declan, to when he said, 'maybe it's not the bunnies I want.' Of course, he wasn't saying that he wanted me, right? Then again, maybe he really was jealous that I went out with Patrick, and if he was, I'm sure it's nothing more than him being a typical guy—he wants what he can't have. But I'm not sure any of that is true, or any of that is logical thinking. He never said he wanted me before, and I'm sure he doesn't now.

But I have no more time to think about that, because as soon as I open the doors to Chatters, I'm greeted by Andrea, the receptionist who quickly informs me that I'm way busier than she first realized. Everyone who called today specifically asked for me.

I glance at the waiting room, and note the pretty women and loud group of children, playing and chatting, and well, just being children. I don't normally do kids cuts, but they all requested me and I'm baffled really.

I call the first child, Scotty, to my chair. He's about nine, and so darn handsome. His little sister Amelia, maybe only two, looks up at him with adoring blue eyes as his mom follows us over.

"Thanks for taking us last minute. We have to get the kids all spiffy up for New Year's."

My heart squeezes a bit, wishing I was better with kids, wishing I could give Declan what he'll eventually want as I put a child's apron on Scotty, and lift the chair.

He laughs. "Whoa, that was fun. Do it again."

I glance at his mom, and she shrugs, so I release the chair and do it again. His laughter fills the salon, and all the other kids look on with happiness, waiting their turns.

"Are you having your daughter's hair done as well?" I ask the lady.

She runs her fingers through her daughter's long curls. "Yes, just a trim."

I glance at my friend Tiffany, who is sitting in her chair, scrolling through her phone. "If you don't want to wait, Tiffany can take her."

"No, we'll wait for you, if that's okay?"

"Sure," I say, and Scotty makes a face when I spray his hair.

"That tickles."

I laugh. "What are you thinking, Scotty? What should we do today?"

"I want a mohawk."

His mom rolls her eyes. "Scotty, we've been over this." She glances at me. "I'm Quinn Long, by the way." I frown, trying to figure out why that name sounds so familiar as I comb Scotty's hair and reach for my scissors. But I can't quite place her, and just assume all these people are here to hit the slopes over the holidays. I trim Scotty's hair, noting that it didn't really need to be cut, and then I move on to her sweet daughter, Amelia.

Once they're done, another little girl named Daisy climbs into the chair, and she's like ten going on sixteen. She tells me exactly what she wants, and how she wants it curled, and I grin at her mother.

Her mother shakes her head. "I'm in trouble, aren't I?"

"I wouldn't know," I say, my heart squeezing with longing. "I don't have kids, and I'm not around them much, but if I had to guess, I'd say yes."

She bursts out laughing and introduces herself as Samantha Reed, and once again, I can't help but think that name sounds familiar. I take my time with Daisy's pretty hair, and she's beaming when I'm done. "You're gorgeous," I tell her.

She smiles at me in the mirror. "So are you."

A weird blush crawls up my cheeks as Samantha grins. "Out of the mouths of babes. Always truthful and honest. You are gorgeous, Nikki."

I smile at the compliment. "Will you be getting your hair done today too?" I check the time. I have one more child to do, then lunch. I didn't check the names for this afternoon, but suspect these mothers are wanting cuts too.

"Yes, we all will be. Sorry we bombarded you like this."

"Chase, it's your turn," one of the moms says and a boy around ten jumps in the chair after Daisy abandons it. Such a cute boy, with big dimples and mischievous eyes.

"Hello Chase, what cut would you like today?"

"I don't want it cut," he complains and crosses his arms. "I want it long. I want to be like Thor."

"Yeah, we all want Thor," his mother mumbles and I keep my smile to myself. "But how about a trim and then later, we can get ice cream."

He grumbles, but quickly comes around. "Okay."

"Great negotiation skills there, Mom."

She winks at me. "I'm a nurse and dealing with adults has given me mad skills to deal with kids." I laugh at that, and she continues with, "I'm Fallon Adams."

Long, Reed, and Adams.

Ohmigod, these are the wives of the Seattle Shooters players. They're all friends of Declan's. What is going on? Why are they here? Getting their hair done by me, nonetheless. The door opens and in walks Declan and my heart jumps into my throat.

"Declan," I murmur. "What are you doing here?"

"Uncle Declan!" The kids scream and run to him. He captures them and gives them all hugs and my heart swells.

"How are my favorite chicken nuggets?"

"We are not chicken nuggets," they all shoot back in protest, and I can't help but grin. It's clear he loves kids. It's all over his face, and the fact that they're all calling him uncle when technically he's not, says so much about their closeness. My stomach knots at the reminder that this is what he wants, and what I can't give him. I'm too afraid to bring kids into this world.

"I see you met the fam," he says as the kids hang off his leg and beg for rides.

"What are you still doing in town?"

He rolls one broad shoulder, and my gaze goes to it. "Have some things to take care of."

I lean into him. "What are your…friends all doing in town?"

"They thought they'd check out Holiday Peak. They didn't believe me that this place goes all out at Christmas, so I invited them to check it out themselves."

"Are their husbands here too?"

"Yeah, they're getting settled at the house. Keeping Mom and Dad company."

I shake my head. "Everyone's going to go crazy. Five members of the Seattle Shooters in town."

"This really is a great town," Quinn says. "I'd love to hit the slopes tomorrow."

"Oh, me too," Sam agrees.

"Me three," Fallon pipes in.

Quinn sighs. "But we did promise the kids we'd take them to the Farmacy." She grins. "Such a cute name for a farm that has pet animals for therapeutic healing. Brilliant, really."

"Oh, I love that place," I say with a laugh. "All the cute animals, and sledding, and snowmobiles. It's great fun. Declan, remember last year when we went and cut a new trail with the snowmobile." I sigh as I remember that afternoon. Declan tearing through the fresh snow while I held onto him from behind, enjoying the feel of his hard body next to mine. As the room goes quiet, I shake my head to pull myself back together. "Anyway, it's a great spot for kids and adults to have fun."

Declan glances at Quinn, then his gaze moves to the other two women, and his eyes light, like he just had an epiphany. "Hey, why don't we take the kids tomorrow, and free the day up for you guys so you can go skiing. Zander was saying he wanted to hit the slopes too. What do you think, Nikki?"

"I...wait...oh, you mean me and you take the kids?"

"Oh my God, really? You guys would do that? That is amazing." Quinn throws her arms around me, and I just stand there and pat her on the back, my mind racing. What just happened here? Quinn lets me go, and Sam and Fallon take turns hugging me, and while it's nice, I'm not sure how I just got roped into taking their kids to the Farmacy. Wait, no that's not true. I know exactly how I got roped into it, and honestly, I shouldn't spend more time with Declan. This is the opposite of what I want. Correction: it's what I want, but the opposite of what my fragile heart needs.

"Mommy, Mommy can we go to the Farmacy with Declan!" Scotty yells, and Quinn hushes him.

"Indoor voice, Scotty, and yes, you can go with Declan and Nikki, only if you promise to behave and keep an eye on your sister."

"I can take care of myself," Amelia says and folds her arms, and I grin at her tenaciousness. She might remind me of well...me when I was a kid.

"I want to hold a baby sheep," Daisy says and cradles her arms, rocking an imaginary baby.

"I want to go sledding," Chase says.

Amelia pushes her way forward. "I want to ride a pony."

"We can do all those things," I find myself saying. Wait, does that mean I just agreed to babysit these four kids for the day? Oh, God, I think I did. Thank God, Declan will be with me. I'm liable to lose one of them in a snowbank.

"How about I take you all to the Chocolate Lab, and give your moms a break."

"Declan, you are the best uncle," Quinn says and hugs him. He puts his arms around her and lifts her clear off the floor. It's easy to tell they're close and I like that he has good friends in Boston.

"You be good, kids," Fallon says, as she hops into my chair, and fluffs her hair up, like she's trying to decide what she'd like done. I use the pedal to lift the chair, and glance at Declan.

"Can I talk to you for a second?" Declan says to Quinn, his words whispered, not meant for my ears, but I can practically read the man's lips I know him so well.

"Yeah," she says and glances at Sam, who's watching them carefully. Sam and Quinn exchange a slight nod, and I can't help but wonder what's going on. Not that it's any of my business. These women are all lovely, but I'm not a part of their tight circle. Another burst of loneliness invades my soul. Growing up, I didn't have a lot of girlfriends. Declan and I were always together, but now that he's gone, I don't really have a girls' support group. I wish I did, though. But Josie Moser, the town's chocolatier, and I have grown close over the last week, and I suspect our relationship will get tighter now that she's dating Declan's best friend.

Declan and Quinn go off to the corner, the kids following them. They lean into one another, talking quietly, intimately, and my heart jumps. Okay, they're tight, close friends, but the way they're leaning into one another and whispering sets alarm bells jangling in my brain.

Is there something going on between the two of them?

DECLAN

Two Days until New Year's Eve:

I wake to the sound of kids playing downstairs, and I instantly smile. The house has been loud since my friends arrived from Boston. As soon as I called Jonah and told him my plan, he gathered everyone he could and they all dropped everything to be here in Holiday Peak with me. While everything is coming together, there is still one detail that is being rushed, and I'm terrified that I won't be able to pull off New Year's Eve the exact way Nikki would want it, even though she has no idea what I'm up to.

"Get up, Uncle Declan," Scotty says, and without knocking, he flings my bedroom door open and barges in. "We want to go to the Farmacy."

"It's only eight in the morning," I inform him. "It doesn't open for two hours, chicken nugget."

"I am not a chicken nugget."

He tugs my blankets off and I'm glad I decided to sleep in pajama pants last night. "What ever happened to privacy?" I ask and put him in a headlock and run my knuckles over his head.

"Chase, help me!" he calls out, laughing, and the next thing I know, there are four kids jumping on my bed and wrestling me. I play with them until someone clears their throat from the door.

I glance up to see Fallon. "Is this how we brush our teeth?" she asks and folds her arms. Her gaze goes to mine. "You're a bad influence."

"What?" I throw my arms up. "I was sound asleep, minding my own business when Scotty burst in here."

"I'm sure you're behind it all," she says with a laugh before zeroing in on the kids. "Now go."

The kids file out of my room, and Fallon stands there like she has something to say. "What?"

"I like her, Declan. We all do."

I smile as I think about my best friend, the woman I want to spend the rest of my life with. "I knew you would."

"We can't wait until she's a part of our family."

I tap the bed and she crosses the room and sits. "I really appreciate you guys dropping everything during the holidays to be here for me."

"There is nowhere else we'd rather be," she says. "Well..." She laughs. "Maybe on the slopes, kid-free for a few hours." She puts her hand on mine. "Are you sure you don't mind taking all four of them? They can be quite the handful."

"I'm looking forward to it." It's true, I am. Someday, I want four or more of my own.

She frowns and goes serious. "You don't think a day with four rambunctious kids will scare Nikki off?"

"I'm hoping for the opposite," I tell her, even though she already knows. I sort of set the whole thing up at Chatters. I lift my gaze as Jamie comes into the room, coffee cup in hand, looking happy and relaxed. He bends to give his wife a kiss and my throat tightens. God, I really want what they have. They fought to get where they are now, and that's exactly what I'm going to do.

"Hey," he says and laughs as he hands me a cup of coffee. "You're going to need a few cups. The kids are still on a sugar high from yesterday's trip to the Chocolate Lab."

I take a much-needed sip. "We're going to have a blast." I wrap my hands around the warm mug and glance at my phone. "So nothing from Kane this morning?"

"It's only five in Seattle. He's got this under control. You can count on him."

I try to ease the tension inside me. "We're really down to the wire."

"He'll be here," he says although he doesn't look as confident as he sounds. "Everything will be ready in time."

"It's a lot to ask." I shake my head. I can't believe how many people have jumped in to help me, working around the clock on all the details. I owe a lot of people when this is over.

"Do you have a backup just in case?" Fallon asks, her nose crinkled.

"No." Shit, should I have thought of something else?

As if sensing my panic, Fallon says, "Don't worry. It will all work out."

I push from the bed as the kids come racing back down the hall after their trip to the bathroom to brush up. They all head downstairs as I check my phone again and make my way to the shower. Two hours later, after a leisurely but loud breakfast, and getting all the kids buckled into Jonah's SUV, we head to Nikki's to pick her up.

She looks unsure as she comes outside and slides into the passenger seat. "Good morning," she says, and four kids start talking at once.

"I think they're pretty excited," I say. "Thanks for doing this with me."

"You say that like I had a choice."

I laugh at that. "You're right. I did spring it on you. Thanks for being a good sport, and honestly, if I have to rustle four kids, you're the girl I want to do it with."

Her body stiffens and she stares straight ahead as I back from her driveway. "You probably should have asked someone with more experience with kids."

"Come on. You're going to love this."

"If I don't?"

"Oh, you want to make a wager, do you?"

She shakes her head. "Bets just get people into trouble."

"You're right," I agree. We drive by town hall, and she frowns.

"I signed up to help decorate for New Year's." she frowns. "Doesn't look like I'm needed this year."

My hands tighten on the wheel. I have the whole town involved in the decorations, and helping me keep her away from the place. Another reason why my friends all made appointments for haircuts yesterday. We need to keep her occupied so she doesn't figure out what's going on. While I hate to keep her in the dark, hate for her to think she's not needed, I'm determined to show her that I do know her, and that when it comes to kids, she has exactly what it takes to be a good mom.

The kids talk and sing and play in the back as we drive, and I glance at Nikki to see how she's taking all the chatter. I find her grinning, and humming along to some song Daisy is playing on her tablet.

"Maybe after today you'll change your mind on having a big family," she teases lightly, but there's something beneath her words, something a little heavy.

"I could say the same thing to you," I shoot back. Her gaze jerks to mine.

"You're saying you think I'll want one?"

I shrug. "Something like that."

She frowns at me, clearly trying to puzzle out what I'm up to, when I pull off the road. "We're here, kids."

Cheers erupt from the back seat as I slowly drive down the long lane, and park beside another SUV.

"Doesn't look too busy," Nikki says.

"That's because it's still the crack of dawn," I tell her and laugh. Mornings and I aren't the best of friends.

"You can stay here and catch up on your beauty sleep if you want," she says. "But I'm going to go have fun."

"You think I'm beautiful," I tease, and the kids all laugh.

"Uncle Declan, you have a big ego," Daisy says, and I glance at her in the mirror.

"Hey where did you ever hear that?"

"Mom says that about all you guys, but she thinks it's funny."

"Do you even know what the word means?" I ask.

Her mouth drops, and she puts a hand on her hips. "Of course, I do. I'm almost a teenager, you know."

"Okay, almost a teenager, let's go see about holding a baby sheep," Nikki says, and opens her door. I follow them out and lock up once the vehicle is empty, and Nikki's steps slow when Amelia takes one of her hands and Daisy takes the other. She glances at me over her shoulder, her eyes wide, almost afraid.

I give her a wink, and gesture with a nod for her to head on in, as I pull my buzzing phone from my pocket, my heart racing when I see it's a text from Kane, letting me know Janice, who is his girlfriend's sister, is finishing the fine details and Kane and Lindsay will be on a flight first thing tomorrow. I glance at the sky and note the darkening clouds. I pray the storm holds off and he has no issues flying here.

I tuck my phone away and hurry to meet up with Nikki and the kids. Will she be losing her mind with the four of them in the few minutes I left them alone, or will she forget that she's afraid of children, afraid of doing the wrong thing, and just enjoy today and have fun? By the time I reach them, I find Nikki and the kids all on their knees. Nikki is whispering quiet words to the baby lamb as she places it in an eager Daisy's hands. Daisy's eyes go wide with happiness.

She coos over the baby and smiles at Nikki. "Do you think I can keep her?"

"No, she lives here," Nikki says gently as she lightly pets the baby. "She needs to be close to her mommy."

Daisy nods in agreement. "You're right. Babies need their mommies. I wouldn't want to be away from mine."

My heart lurches and I go still as I listen to the exchange—totally understanding the loss Nikki suffered so many years ago. But not having a mother doesn't mean she won't be a good mother, and that's what today is all about. She's already growing comfortable with these four chicken nuggets.

As if feeling my eyes on her, Nikki's head lifts, and her eyes latch onto mine. She gives me a small smile and gestures with a nod for me to join them. I drop down next to Nikki, and Amelia shuffles until she's on my lap. Nikki draws in air at the sight, and I put my arms around Amelia to hold her tight.

"Do you want to hold her too?" I ask.

Amelia nods, and I hold her arms out to show her how to cradle the baby sheep. Daisy gently places the lamb into Amelia's arms and Amelia practically cries.

"I want to keep her," she says, and we all go quiet as she strokes the baby.

I consider what to say, how to console her, when Chase blurts out, "I want to go on the snowmobiles."

His outburst eases the tension, and we all laugh. "I can only take one at a time," I explain and glance at Nikki. "Do you maybe want to stay here, or go sledding while I take turns giving them rides?"

"I want to stay here with Nikki," Daisy says.

"Me too," Amelia agrees, always siding with the older Daisy.

"Nikki?"

She crinkles her nose. "You sure you trust me?"

"More than anything," I say, and something passes over her pretty eyes, something that looks like love. I take a breath, but it's hard to fill my lungs as everything I feel for her jumps to the surface, and honest to God, waiting two more days to show her that I do indeed know her might just be the death of me. All I want to do is take her to my bed and take care of her, the way I should have been doing for years.

"I think us girls will be just fine."

The girls nestle in next to her as the baby lamb makes a noise and they all laugh. "Okay boys, follow me."

I head out, and give one last glance over my shoulder, and my heart beats a little harder in my chest as I see her bond with Daisy and Amelia, just like I knew they would. For the next hour, I give the boys each a turn on the snowmobile, carving out new paths in the fresh snow, and they both love it. When our hour is up, we head off to find the girls, and they're racing each other down the hill, and I swear to God, I could sob with happiness when their squeals of laughter reach my ears. I want this. I want all of this. With the gorgeous woman waving wildly at me. My heart stills in my chest as her sled races toward Amelia, an accident in the making. She must read the terror on my face, because the next thing I know she's tearing her focus from me, jerking her body to the left, and getting dumped head first into the trees.

NIKKI

ne Day until New Year's Eve:

OMG, I am still so embarrassed.

"I'm fine," I say for the hundredth time, and adjust the bag of semi-frozen peas on my forehead—even though I no longer need them—but Declan's teammates and their wives and kids won't stop fussing over me. Declan brought me back to his place yesterday after I tumbled off the sled and banged my head. He insisted that Fallon check me over. When everyone came back from the slopes, they started fretting over me and here it is well into the next day and they're still doing it.

Of course, I didn't mind Declan fussing last night, not when he took me to his bed and insisted on sleeping next to me, just to be cautious, you know, in case I needed him in the middle of the night. I needed him, but in ways that would surely shock the hell out of him. Yeah, ways that meant his hands and mouth were on my body. God, I wish I didn't love the way he held me tight to his hard chest, like I was his, forever. But we're friends, and it's what we'll always be.

You want more.

Of course, I want more. I just can't have it and when he finally does leave after the holidays, I'm going to have to find the strength to move forward. Daisy comes running into the room and plunks herself down beside me.

"Oh, Nikki," she says, all grown up-like. "You poor girl."

I chuckle at that as she takes the peas from my hand and gingerly presses them to the goose egg on my forehead, which has shrunk significantly since last night. I glance at the little cutie next to me. Here I thought one of them would end up in the ditch, when I landed there myself. It was either that or crash into Amelia. The last thing I was going to do was hurt her. Flinging myself into the trees was the only option, and to be honest, up until that moment, I really enjoyed hanging out with them.

Chase comes into the room, carrying a plate of cookies, walking slowly to balance them. He sits on the other side of me, and holds the plate out. "Want one?"

He's such a sweet and kind little boy. If I had a son, I'd want him to be like Chase, or even Scotty. If I had a girl, I want her to be like Daisy, or Amelia. Great, now I'm not only going to miss Declan, I'm going to miss all his hockey family too. That's what these people are to him. Family. I can't deny that there's a huge part of me that wants in on that.

"Thanks, Chase, but I'm good." He shrugs, and starts eating the cookies.

Quinn sits on the coffee table across from me. "Thanks for taking the kids yesterday. I'm sorry it ended the way it did, but they still loved it. They love you, obviously," she says as Amelia crawls onto my lap, and cups my cheeks.

"Are you feeling better, Aunt Nikki?" she asks.

My throat tightens as she calls me her aunt. "I am," I tell her. She leans in, kisses my nose, and shimmies off my lap to go play with her brother Scotty, who is deep into a puzzle. He pats her on the head like she's a puppy and I grin. Big brother Scotty is a lot older than Amelia and I do wonder about the huge age gap.

I sigh with a kind of longing that I've been able to keep buried for years, but now after being with the kids, it's banging on the door, demanding to be answered. "The kids are all sweet. I loved getting to know them. They all have such unique personalities."

"You're going to be a good mom," she tells me and my heart squeezes so tight, tears pound behind my eyes, and it hurts to swallow.

"I never planned on having kids."

"Don't be silly," Daisy says adjusting the nearly thawed pea bag. "Every mom has a kid."

I crinkle my nose as I think about that and Quinn laughs. "Daisy, why don't you go help Amelia and Scotty with the puzzle." I take the bag from Daisy and she skips across the room. Chase finishes his cookies and darts back into the kitchen for more, and I laugh as Declan's mom sneaks him another one.

When we're alone, Quinn says, "You don't want kids?" She holds her hands up. "Sorry, that's none of my business, it's just that you're so good with them."

I go quiet for a long time. Over the years, memories of my mom have faded, and I struggle so hard to hang on to them. One of our last memories was us in the attic, going through old boxes. I'd found her wedding dress and tried it on. We'd laughed and played dress up and pretended I was getting married. Of course, back then Declan was obviously the groom, represented by a broom handle. It was later that year we lost Mom, and many years after that, we lost all those boxes too, thanks to a huge winter storm that tore part of the roof off and flooded our keepsakes with rainwater.

"I lost my mom when I was young," I tell her. "I never thought I could be a good mom, never thought I had what it took, since I was raised by my father, and was always a tomboy."

She shifts closer and takes my hand. "I'm sorry, Nikki. Declan did tell me that. I hope you don't mind that he shared something private and painful."

"I don't mind," I say. But why on earth would that come up in conversation?

Quinn puts her hand over her stomach. "I lost a baby many years ago. I had a miscarriage between Scotty and Amelia. It was rough and not something you ever get over."

"I'm so sorry." I squeeze her hand. "I didn't know."

She nods. "We waited a few years to try again, and now we have sweet Amelia, but loss is hard, any kind of loss. The loss of a child...the loss of a parent when you're only a child..." Her voice falls off and we both go quiet for a moment. "I wasn't sure we'd ever have another child and of course, I blamed myself for the miscarriage, figuring I did something wrong."

I lean toward her, understanding the pain of loss and blame. "You didn't."

She nods. "I know. We went to counselling. We found a way to move past our fears and move forward. We're happy."

I smile at her, my heart thudding. I was a fool to think there might be something between Declan and Quinn. They're just good friends and whatever they were talking about was none of my business, although I do feel a twinge of jealousy. He used to always talk to me.

"You all look so happy."

Her smile is warm, when she says, "You look happy when you're with Declan."

Every muscle in my body tenses. "He's my best friend, Quinn."

"I know, but you want more," she states.

"What makes you say that?"

She turns to make sure we're alone, then leans in closer. "I can see the way you look at him, and the way he looks at you."

"You think he looks at me like—"

The front door flings open and in rushes Brody and Josie. Josie darts into the living room. "Nikki are you okay? I'm sorry I didn't get here sooner. Declan messaged Brody a little bit ago, but we were elbow deep in chocolate."

"I'm fine," I say, happy to see her, but hating the interruption. Was Quinn trying to tell me Declan looked at me with love in his eyes? Is it possible that I refused to see it because I didn't think I could give him what he needed? God, if that's true, and I accused him of not knowing me, it must have really hurt him.

Josie sits next to me, her gaze moving over my face. She winces, and makes a hissing sound. "This isn't good."

"It's okay, it's going down."

She studies my face. "Let's hope it's gone before tomorrow night. You don't want to be photographed with—"

Quinn clears her throat loudly, and I don't miss the way her foot nudges Josie's, or the way Josie abruptly stopped talking, and now looks mortified.

"What pictures, what's going on?" I glance past Quinn's shoulders and spot Declan and Brody in deep conversation, both guys checking their phones.

"I just mean New Year's Eve pictures," Josie says. "At the town hall celebration. We all want to look our best for the pictures, right?"

"Speaking of the town hall. I have to go. I'm supposed to help decorate." I'm about to push off the sofa, when they both stop me, shoving me back down.

"It's all done," Josie blurts out. "Completely decorated. I helped out last night. No need for you to go there."

"I wouldn't mind looking, to make sure nothing is missing. I've been part of the decorating crew for as long as I can remember."

"Nope, no need. It's all good," Josie assures me.

Why is everyone acting so strange? Is there a full moon coming? Or maybe the 'magic snow' is making everyone a little crazy, because it's coming down hard right now. Jonah and Zander join Declan and Brody in the hall, and they're all talking quietly, about something that looks rather serious.

"What's going on?" I ask.

Quinn glances over her shoulder. "Oh, they're worried about Kane and his girlfriend Lindsay. They're flying in tomorrow, and the weather isn't looking great."

"Flying in from where?"

"Seattle?"

"What for?"

"I guess they want to do some skiing," Quinn says, and I shake my head.

"Don't they have amazing ski hills in Seattle?"

"Yeah, sure but come on, this is Holiday Peak, who doesn't want to be here for the holidays?" I turn to Josie, and note the chocolate on her face.

"You have a bit," I say and reach out to swipe it away. She shakes her head.

"When don't I have chocolate on my face?"

"I thought you were closing for a few days."

She glances down, like she's in thought. "Yeah, I uh...was making a chocolate fountain for the New Year's Eve party."

"Oh, I love those."

Her head lifts and she flashes a wide smile. "I know."

"How do you know that?" I mean we've grown closer, but I don't think I've ever told anyone that before.

Quinn clears her throat and Josie's eyes go wide again. "Oh, everyone loves a chocolate fountain. That's all I meant." She jumps up. "I'm going to go say hello to Declan's parents."

"Good idea," Quinn says with a grin.

I watch her hurry off like her pants are on fire. "Is she okay? She's acting strange."

Quinn smiles at me. "New love, it messes with the brain."

Fallon comes back into the room. "Josie mentioned you wanted to go over to the town hall. I don't think that's a good idea. You need to rest until the bump is completely gone."

"I feel perfectly fine, Fallon."

She pulls a pen flashlight from her pocket and checks my eyes again. "I think you need to give it another day."

"I'm not used to sitting around. I'm going to go crazy."

"Let's all play a game of cards then," Quinn suggests.

The next thing I know, we're all seated at the table, playing crazy eights with the kids. The guys left ten minutes ago. Declan said they were going to check on the hall to put my worries at ease, although he's only managed to do the opposite. Everyone is acting strange—even me. Here I am hanging out with the players' wives and kids. Not only am I loving every minute of it, I'm thinking about how much the kids would love the pony rides I promised, and how I can get them back to the Farmacy. Maybe I wouldn't be a bad mom.

Maybe it's time I moved past my fears because I want this. I want all of this. With Declan.

Now I just have to figure out what he wants.

9

DECLAN

New Year's Eve:

With the entire town working to keep Nikki away from the town hall, and the girls keeping her busy with 'girl' stuff at Nikki's place—getting their nails, makeup and hair done for tonight's event, I jump in the car with Brody, and carefully back out of the driveway. But with the snow falling heavily, I'm not certain Kane and Lindsay's plane will be able to land, and the key piece to proving to Nikki that I do indeed know her, and damn well love her, is in their luggage. Lindsay's sister dropped everything for me, and I owe her big time for this. Thank God I reached out to friends and they were able to help me pull this off. I'd be lost without them.

I turn the wipers to high, and creep through the streets, and suddenly from behind, a siren sounds and lights fill the dark night. "Shit, I'm going under the speed limit. Why are we being pulled over? We don't have time for this."

"I don't know, just pull over and we'll find out."

I ease the car off the road, and Patrick pulls over behind me. I crack my window as he approaches, the snow quickly accumulating on his shoulders and hat.

"What's up, Patrick?" I ask. Is he pissed about my plan, because I'm pretty sure everyone in town knows it by now?

"I called for a plow to go ahead of you, so you get to the airport safely. I'm going to follow from behind."

What the hell? "You...why are you doing all this?"

"Because Jesus, Declan. You and Nikki belong together, and I want to see it happen as much as everyone else in town does."

"So you're not pissed at me for coming between you two?"

"I like Nikki. She's sweet and gorgeous and so kind, but we can only ever be friends. We quickly realized that." He grins. "Besides, I kind of met someone."

I chuckle. "Yeah, I thought so. I'm happy for you, man."

A big plow comes from behind and pulls in front of me. Patrick taps the roof of my car. "Okay, go carefully, and I'm right behind you the whole way."

"Let's just hope the plane can land."

"Fingers crossed," Patrick says before he heads back to his truck. I shut the window and turn on the heater.

Brody grins at me. "Only in a small town does shit like that happen."

"Get used to it. Now that you're with Josie, you'll be spending a lot of time here too."

"Can't wait."

I carefully follow the plow truck. "Any updates?" I ask, as Brody scrolls through his phone, continually refreshing the incoming flights.

"Still says delay."

"Shit."

Quinn helped me put a backup plan together, and while it's a last-minute fix, what I have in mind will simply make it perfect. I tap the steering wheel and focus on the road ahead, and my heart is so full at the way this entire town rallied around me to help. Everyone loves Nikki, me included, and we all want her happy. Fingers crossed that what I've set up will do just that.

We creep our way to the airport, and what is usually a twenty-minute drive turns into an hour, and with the clock ticking, I try not to panic. We finally make it, but the flight status hasn't changed.

I park and Patrick pulls in beside me. I guess he's going to wait to escort us all back. I give him a wave and Brody and I head inside, to pace the wide expanse of floor, like everyone else waiting on flights.

Minutes tick by and soon enough the board changes, alerting us that the flight has landed. Two seconds later I get a text from Kane to let me know they've touched down. I turn to Brody, and we throw our arms around each other. When we realize people are starting to notice us, we smile and prepare ourselves for the onslaught of selfies.

The crowd doesn't disappoint, and we take pictures until Kane and Lindsay appear with their luggage. I grab hold of Kane and hug him, pulling Lindsay in with me.

"You guys are the best."

"Wait until you see it, Declan," Lindsay says, her eyes wide. "My sister did an exact replica. It's gorgeous."

My throat tightens with excitement and gratitude. "I owe her. Big time."

"Oh, don't worry." She winks at me. "She expects payment. Big time."

I laugh at that. "Anything she wants." I put my arm around Lindsay. "Come on, let's get out of here." We hurry through the crowd, and trudge through the snow. Back at the car, we all pile in, and I nod to Patrick. The plow is waiting off to the side and when I start the vehicle it pulls ahead of me, while the sheriff follows.

"Wow, that's some service you got here, Declan," Kane says with a laugh.

We joke for a moment, then Lindsay talks excitedly about meeting Nikki, and seeing my small town as I drive, and Brody tells her about the skiing, the Farmacy, Christmas Land, and all the other fun things to do every holiday season. Lindsay asks about Josie, and because he's a man in love, he talks nonstop about her the whole way home, telling them the story of how he nearly screwed everything up.

Kane grins. "People falling in love left, right and center. Must be something in the well water."

By the time we reach home and I glance at the clock, panic sets in. "We don't have much time. We'll have to dress fast."

"Don't worry. I can dress fast," Lindsay says. "I'm pretty low maintenance and I'm just so excited to be here." We hop from the car, and I help them with the luggage. We kick the snow off our boots, before we step inside the house to find Mom and Dad, Zander, Jonah and Jamie all dressed and ready to go. "Is the babysitter here?" I ask when I hear Daisy ordering the kids around in the other room.

"Hi Declan," Tracy calls out from the living room. Tracy is one of the four kids who live next door. She's home from college for the holidays, and stepped up to help when we asked. "Congratulations," she says.

"A little early for that, but I'll take it," I say under my breath.

Lindsay opens her suitcase and gingerly hands me over the black vinyl garment bag. "Here it is."

I hold it carefully, like it's a newborn baby. So much work went into the design, I'm afraid to wrinkle or rip something.

"Are you going to look?" Lindsay asks.

I want to see what's in it, but I also don't. "Isn't that considered bad luck?" Honestly, I need all the luck on my side tonight.

"You're right. Don't open it."

"Head on up and get ready, you guys," Mom says, shooing us all away. "Quinn texted and they're trying to stall Nikki. She's asking questions. She knows something is up." She shakes her head. "She told Sam she was going outside for air, and Mabel caught her walking toward the town hall. Thank God she managed to turn her around."

Dad laughs. "Hard to keep a secret in this town."

"Unless the entire town is in on it," I say.

Mom holds her hands out for the garment bag and I hand it over, then follow my friends upstairs while the others wait in the front entrance for us, everyone pacing restlessly. I go to my closet to take out my tux. I take one moment to stand there, the reality of what I'm about to do crashing over me. We're not in Tuscany on a beach—Nikki's dream destination —but it's sure going to feel like it. I dress fast, run a comb through my hair and hurry back down the stairs. The nervous energy in the house wraps around me, and I begin to chew on my nails as I pace.

"Relax, Declan. Tonight is going to be perfect," my mom says and cups my cheeks.

"I don't want to be late."

"She waited for you this long." She winks. "I'm sure she won't mind a few more minutes."

I take a fast breath as my heart pounds. "I almost lost her, Mom," I say, and choke on my words. I never, ever should have kept Nikki waiting for anything.

"You didn't, and that's all that matters now." I glance at Dad, who is smiling at me, letting me know he's behind me all the way and I'm so grateful to have such loving parents. I take a breath, and let it out slowly, working to relax myself.

Brody, Kane and Lindsay come down, and Jamie, Zander and Jonah come from the kitchen. I take a moment to think about how lucky I am. "Thanks for being here, guys. I..."

"Save the speech for later, buddy," Brody says with a laugh as he claps me on the back. "We need to go."

I scoop up the vinyl, zippered garment bag, and we split up between two vehicles, and head to the town hall, and my heart swells when I see all the vehicles. I think everyone in Holiday Peak is here to witness the big event, and I pray it goes off without a hitch. I swallow the lump punching into my throat when I get inside, and I can hardly believe we all pulled this off. The place is gorgeous, and Nikki is going to love it.

"They're on their way," Brody says and holds his phone out. "Josie just messaged me."

"Thanks, man," I say, breathless, frightened, and excited all at the same time.

"You've got this, Declan."

"Yeah, thanks."

Brody gives my shoulder a squeeze. "I know people get nervous on their wed—"

"Shit!"

"What?" Brody's head rears back.

I glance at the black bag. "I have to hang this before she gets here, and I don't want to look at it."

He nods. "That's what best buds are for, right? I'm not just another pretty face, dude. I'm here to help."

I laugh at that as he takes the bag from me and pulls down the zipper. I slam my eyes shut. "I don't want to see it," I repeat.

"Stay here, then. I'll get it hung up, so she can see it when she comes in."

The din of the crowd grows louder as Brody goes to the hall with the bag in hand. A minute later, he runs back to me, excitement and nervousness on his face as he straightens his bowtie. "They're here. Get into position."

Everyone moves, some remain standing, some take a seat, and I go still, drawing in a big breath and holding it as the women walk into the hall. I don't think Nikki is with them and for a second, I panic. But she steps inside, takes one fast look at the décor, the food, and chocolate fountain, then turns to me as I drop to one knee and hold out a velvet box.

"Nikki," I say, and work to keep my voice steady as I take pleasure in the sight of her, dressed in a form-fitting black cocktail dress that showcases her sweet curves. Possession wells up inside of me and I suddenly want to stand, hide her from every man in the room, but that's crazy. Crazy. Yeah, but that's what I am. Crazy in love with this woman. I have been since we were kids and it's well past time since I did something about it.

"Declan," she says her voice a low soft whisper full of shock and confusion. "What's...what's going on?" Her head lifts and she glances past my shoulder to take in the crowd. She falters backwards a tiny bit, and I shuffle closer, and open the box to show her the ring I had made for her. It's not an engagement ring or a wedding ring. No, it's a daisy ring, fashioned after her favorite flower.

"I love you," I say, those three little words coming straight from my heart. Three little words I should have told her many years ago. "Will you marry me?"

She stands there staring at me for one long second, tears pooling in her eyes, and my heart hammers as she blinks rapidly, like she's trying to wrap her brain around all this. And why wouldn't she be confused? But now, as she frowns at me, deep in thought—and I really wish I knew what she was thinking—I start to pray, worried that I made a mistake. Then when she says those three little words...the three little words no man wants to hear...I know I fucked up.

NIKKI

"Declan...what...no!" I practically shout, my voice bordering on hysteria. A collective gasp sounds in the room, then it falls silent and I lift my head, take in all the eyes staring at me in shock. My stomach clenches, and I can't get air as I scan the hall. It's decorated beautifully, but it's not our usual winter New Year's Eve theme. No, it's decorated in light airy colors, a beach theme, and my God, I'm sure there's even sand sprinkled on the floor, under a gazebo, designed for a wedding. "What have you done?" I ask.

"Nikki," he says, his voice low and strained. I back up a bit, stumble really, and that's when I turn to grab the back of a chair behind me. But the second I twist, and see a gorgeous white dress hanging from a hook, the world goes dark around me, and a cry lodges in my throat.

"Declan," I cry out and the next thing I know I'm in his arms.

"I've got you."

I let him hold me, sob into his chest as years of stifled emotions flood me. The room is so silent, save for my cries, and embarrassment grips me. "Declan, please. Everyone's watching me."

"Come with me."

He scoops me up, and our friends part to make a path as he carries me into a private back room. A second later, I'm sitting on a chair, and he's crouched down in front of me, worry and fear all over his handsome face.

"Nikki, I'm sorry." He runs a shaky hand through his hair. "I think I went about this all wrong, but I wanted to show you that I do know you, and that I do love you. I shocked you… you weren't ready for this. I should have talked to you, but words…I wanted to show you."

As he rambles on, one word—love—sticks in my brain.

I put my hand on his shoulder to stop him from talking and when his words fall off and his gaze settles on mine, I ask, "You love me?"

"Of course, I love you. I've always loved you." I sit there for one long second, and shake my head as I absorb his words. He inches back, his gaze searching my face. "You don't believe me?"

"This isn't what you want." I wave my hand around. "This isn't what you ever wanted. I know you care about me, but you saw me with Patrick, and I'm guessing you didn't like not having me to yourself. You pretty much told me you were jealous, Declan. I passed it off as typical behavior. Wanting what you suddenly can't have."

"No, you're wrong." He tugs on his hair again. "Well, okay you're right. I hated not having you to myself, and maybe seeing you with Patrick was the ass kicking I needed." He takes my hand, and his warmth seeps under my skin. I lean into him, my heart pounding with everything I feel for him. "Nikki, you're my best friend, and all these years, I was terrified of doing something or saying something to mess things up between us. I love you, I want to be with you, and there were times I thought you wanted that too, but then you'd pull back. You always pulled back." He takes a breath, and continues. "It used to confuse the hell out of me, but it doesn't anymore. I know what you're afraid of."

"You do?"

"Yes, you're terrified of being a mother. Terrified of something happening to you, of leaving a child behind, because you know how painful it is to lose a mother. But life is short, babe, we both know that, and we have to push past our fears and take chances. Your mother died young in a tragic accident. That doesn't mean it's going to happen to you, and you're going to be an amazing mother."

His words ping around in my rattled brain, and as I shake my head to settle it, I say, "You...brought your friends here, with their kids on purpose, didn't you?" I sniff, and he brushes a tear from my cheek. "I mean, not just because you had all this planned." I glance toward the door closing us in, and the town folks out. "But because you wanted me to hang out with their kids, right?"

"Yeah, I wanted you to see it wasn't so scary."

"It wasn't," I say and give him a small smile. "I really like them."

"They like you too."

I glance down, my pulse pounding at the base of my throat. "You love me, Declan?"

"God, yes. I fucking love you," he says as tears pulse behind my eyes. He waves his hand. "All this was to show you how much. Your dream wedding is on a beach in Tuscany. I couldn't pull that off, but we did the best we could to replicate a beach."

"I never told you about Tuscany."

"You didn't need to."

I put my hands on his face. "It's beautiful."

"We have tickets for a honeymoon in Tuscany. I can't go until after the NHL season. I know you waited long enough, and—"

"And I'll wait longer for you, Declan. I'll wait as long as it takes, now that I know you love me."

He shimmies closer, and moves between my legs. "I know why you went out with Patrick."

I swallow, hard. "I couldn't do this...us...anymore. I love you. I always have. But watching you walk away time after time, and knowing I was afraid I couldn't give you what you wanted anyway... I had to find a way to move on."

"You love me?"

"Of course, I love you, you big goof."

"I'm never walking away from you again, Nikki, and we can make our home wherever you want. I know you don't want to leave your dad so we can stay here during the off season, or maybe we can take your dad with us to wherever we live. You might want to be in Boston, or we could go to Seattle. We can go wherever you want."

"I think Dad wants to go to Florida," I say with a laugh. "And I'm okay living anywhere, as long as it's with you." His lips twitch, and another bout of unease rolls through me. I frown and twist my fingers.

"Hey, what?"

"I just want you to be sure. I mean...Patrick."

"You see this ring," he says and opens the box to show me a gorgeous, one-of-a-kind daisy ring, and my throat clenches as more tears fall. "I had this made for you last summer. It was your Christmas present. I never got a chance to give it to you. This ring was long before Patrick."

"You always give me silly gag gifts."

"I know. I'm an idiot. I was scared to send the wrong message, but this ring, I was going to give it to you on Christmas Eve..." He pauses and shakes his head. "It was a message and I was going to wait to see if you received it. If you laughed it off, I would have laughed it off. If you realized it meant I loved you—and you were happy about that—I would have told you how much I loved you. It shouldn't have been all up to you, but I was afraid to come right out and tell you how I felt. I was a chicken shit, and I'm done with that."

I bite my lip. "Maybe you should have to wear those chicken leg socks you got me, then."

"If that's what it takes to prove I love you, I will."

My entire body warms as I think about the effort he went through to prove to me how much he loves me. "I think you've proved it, Declan, and I'm sorry. I never should have said you didn't know me, and this ring—"

"I'll get you a real wedding band and a diamond engagement ring. Whatever you want."

I shake my head. "No, this is perfect. It's the only ring I want. I love it, but I have to tell you, I got you heated socks for Christmas. Nothing as elaborate."

"See that's the thing, Nikki. You're sweet and thoughtful, and those socks mean a lot. They mean you care about me. You've been taking care of your father, me, yourself and everyone else in this town for as long as I can remember. I want to be the one taking care of you."

Tears spill down my cheeks, and Declan cups my face and brings my lips to his. His kiss is warm, soft, full of love and passion. "I love you," I murmur as my heart swells inside my chest.

He holds out the box. "Can we try this again?" I shake my head no and his face falls, fear in his eyes. "Nikki."

"Let's do it out there, like you'd originally planned," I say quickly to put his worries to rest. "I'm sure everyone is dying to know what's going on."

A huge, relieved smile spreads across his beautiful face. "Okay, I like that."

He stands, and pulls me up with him and that's when it hits me. "Declan!"

He goes completely stiff. "What?"

"The dress. Ohmigod, the dress is a replica of my mother's."

"I know. I hope you like it."

I begin to sob, and he pulls me to him. "I never told you… how did you know?"

"I know you, Nikki. I know everything about you. I know what you want, what your fears are and what you need. I'm going to be here for everything from now on. I promise you that."

I go up on my tip toes and press my lips to his. "How did you do it?"

"My buddy Kane. He's out there, you'll meet him. His girlfriend Lindsay is too, and I can't wait for you to meet her too. Anyway, Lindsay's sister is a costume designer and I sent a picture of the dress. The picture you have on the mantel, and she dropped everything to do this for me…for us."

I shake my head, shocked and deeply touched. "I can't believe you managed to pull this all off in such a short period of time."

"I called in a lot of favors and will be paying until I'm ninety, for sure."

I throw my arms around him, and as I hug him, that's when something else occurs to me. "Declan!" I shout again. "You want me to marry you."

"Uh, yeah, you're just figuring that out," he teases.

I whack him. "No, I mean right now. You want me to marry you right now."

"Yeah, I do."

I go quiet, and let my gaze roam over his handsome face. Declan Bradbury, NHL superstar. My best friend. My fiancé. My soon-to-be husband.

"I do too," I say, and he picks me up and spins me around.

"Let's go say that in front of our family and friends."

Declan sets me down, and with our faces somber, he opens the door and everyone falls silent, all eyes on us, waiting patiently. Declan's hand finds mine and he gives it a squeeze as he takes me to the center of the room, and goes down on one knee. I can no longer keep the smile from my face, and little gasps of joy spread through the room.

He opens the box, and holds it out. "Nikki, I love you with all my heart. Will you marry me and make me the happiest man on the planet? Here, tonight. In front of all our friends and family?"

I take a big breath, and soak in the moment. I have never been happier in my life, but this is just the beginning of a lifetime of love and laughter, family and friends.

"Yes," I say, and everyone starts clapping.

He takes the ring and puts it on my finger. As I admire it, he stands, and lightly kisses me. Just then Dad steps up to me, Carol behind him. "I love you, kiddo," he says, and I throw my arms around him.

"I love you too, Dad."

He laughs. "Now I can finally move to Florida." He leans in and whispers, "Carol likes the idea of Florida too." I laugh and hug him. Over his shoulder I spot Patrick and Violet, and they both give me a big smile. As they do, I can't help but think Mabel was right, and Christmas snow really is magical.

Dad steps away, and Declan says. "Go put your dress on, babe, I can't wait to make you mine."

I nod, and hold my left hand out. "A daisy." A little chuckle bubbles up in my throat. "Here I thought you couldn't get daisies in Holiday Peak during the winter."

"Who says you can't get daisies in the winter."

"What?"

He waves his arm and that's when I realize all the flowers in the room are daisies. Hundreds of them. "Declan..." It's the only word I can get out through a tight throat.

"Nikki," he begins, his voice low, hoarse, like he's fighting back tears, too. "I know your mom can't be here with us today, but the flowers, the dress, it's a way of having her with us." His eyes water as he puts his hand over my heart. "In here."

Fresh tears fall down my cheeks, and that's when I notice there isn't a dry eye in the place. "Thank you, Declan. Thank you for thinking of her, and making sure she's with us on this special day."

"I always want her with us," he says, and then scrunches up his face. "Well, maybe not on our honeymoon, or later tonight when we consummate this marriage. That would be weird."

A laugh bubbles up inside me, all the love I have for Declan and this entire town flooding my heart with happiness.

He slaps my backside. "Dress. Now. Move it. I can't wait another minute."

I turn and glance at him over my shoulder. "Maybe I'll take my time, make you wait for a change."

His grin is sexy, mischievous. "Just so you know, I've been waiting too, but whatever you want, babe. I'll wait until the end of time if it means you'll be mine. But just remember. The sooner you get in that dress, the sooner I get you out of it."

The entire room breaks out in laughter, and heat crawls into my cheeks, but I love his playfulness. I love him, and plan to spend the rest of my life proving it by giving him the family he always wanted—what I was afraid to want—but with him by my side I have nothing to fear. My steps slow as happiness seeps deeper into my heart.

"Nikki," he growls. "Move it."

"I'm moving. I'm moving!"

***'

Thank you so much for reading, **The Sweet Talker**, book 11 in my **Players on Ice**. I hope you loved this story as much as I loved writing it. Keep reading for an excerpt of **Fair Play Book 1, in my End Zone series.**

If you love sport romances, check out Fair Play

ELLA:

"What does this button do?"

I smack my best friend's hand away from the football's team brand new camcorder, and give her the evil eye. She knows better than to play with it, which makes the shocked looked on her face all the more amusing. But the fact is, I've been entrusted with the very expensive device to record the Falcons' first home game. Since I can't afford to replace it, I can't let my friend go around poking at every shiny knob and possibly breaking something.

"What?" Peyton says, blinking dark lashes over big innocent eyes. "I'm just asking a question."

"No. You're pushing buttons you shouldn't be pushing. Now sit there before I send you to the bleachers with everyone else." I point to the bench to the left of us and raise a warning brow.

She gives a light laugh, brushing off my threat. "You'd never do that. You love me too much." She's right. I wouldn't. Peyton and I have been best friends since kindergarten, and for the last three years we've been college roommates choosing apartment-style living over a sorority house. She's here for a degree in social work, and I'm here because I want to be a filmmaker. Yeah, working in Hollywood, behind the scenes, has been my dream since childhood.

Beside me, Peyton gives a very big, very happy sigh and takes in the football field from our perch—only the best, first class seating for the camera woman. "I do love the perks of being your best friend," she says as she admires the football players warming up. A few are so close we could practically reach out and touch them if we wanted to. I don't.

"I really can't understand the fascination," I murmur. "A bunch of guys in tight pants chasing a ball."

She crosses her arms, and waggles her brows at me. "What's it called again when a player passes the goal line with the ball in his hand?"

"Winning," I say, giving her a look that suggests she might be dense, but when she breaks out laughing, I crack a smile. Yeah, I get it. I'm the one who's dense. It's true, I know nothing about football, but I need this fourth-year credit to complete my cinematic arts degree and really, do I need to understand the game to record it for the team to analyze later? That would be a big fat no. I hope.

"Well, at least you know how this thing works," Peyton says, once again scoping out the buttons on my camcorder. "How about this knob? What does it do?"

"Peyton, cut it out." I slap her hand again and laugh at her childish antics. How we remained friends all these years when we're so different is a mystery. But we love each other like sisters. Sisters? Wait, that's not right at all. I'm an identical twin and my sister Ivy and I go together like hotdogs and Ferris wheels. Peyton and I, however, no matter how different, we just work.

I stare at her. "Don't you have football players to drool over?" Unlike me, she knows every player, and doesn't hold the same kind of grudge against them as I do.

I adjust my ballcap to shade the sun from my eyes as I glance out at the football field. I catch sight of my sister Ivy as she kicks one leg out and flirts with one of the players, trailing her finger over his chest. Blonde and bubbly. That's Ivy. We were raised by the same two parents, yet we're so different, and I wouldn't be caught dead in a cheerleading outfit that barely covered my ass. That's her business though, and I don't judge or interfere in her life, just like she doesn't interfere in mine.

I'd like to think when push comes to shove, she'd be there for me, just like I'd be there for her. At least, I think she'd be there for me. We might not hang out, but we love one another and have each other's best interests at heart. Of that I'm certain. It's funny really. Ever since we were young, we fell into certain roles. The extrovert and the introvert, the outgoing one and the quiet one. I always stood in the shadows and let her have the limelight. Pretty Ivy, the theater student who lights up a room with her smile and flamboyance when she enters. Which of course, makes me the introverted smart, quiet one. We both easily fell into those roles and have yet to stray.

Peyton gives a low, slow whistle. "I don't know what you have against tight pants. Look at all those cute butts and luscious muscles. Talk about slurpalicious." She rakes her teeth over her bottom lip. "Don't you want one little nibble, one taste?"

I give her a playful shove to move her away from the camcorder. "No. No nibbles. No tastes." I'm a virgin with no plans to change that anytime soon, and as my best friend, she damn well knows it. I take up position behind the camera, and look at the world through my beloved lens. I exhale a contented breath. This is where I belong. This is where I feel most at home.

Okay, yeah, so it's true. I'm the world's biggest nerd. Do I care? Nope. Not one little bit. I'm happy to stand in the shadow and view the world through my camcorder lens. As I do, I catch sight of Ivy again as she shakes her ass for the boys on the field. Truth be told, I actually hate football players. Back in high school, they bullied my friend Jacob until he ended up taking his own life. Terrible hazing went on at our school. The bullying was torturous and cruel, and no matter how hard Peyton and I tried to help Jacob, get him help, the bullying continued, and actually increased the more we tried to stop it. A stab of pain sears my heart at the painful memory, and I suck in air to breathe through it. I know I shouldn't lump all jocks into one category, shouldn't label them all as egotistical bullies, but a single player has yet to prove me wrong. Arrogant assholes. What more can I say?

I check my watch, as my stomach growls. "Hungry much?" Peyton says. "Maybe you'd like a nibble after all?"

"Really, Peyton. Did you just meet me?" I tease and reach into my backpack and grab a granola bar, all the while trying to cleanse my brain of football players and their tight asses—one player in particular. Peyton holds her hand out, and I place a bar in her palm. Granola bars and juice boxes on the go. The life of a busy fourth year student—or that of a toddler.

She tears into her wrapper and looks me in the eye. Her brow is furrowed as she examines me like I'm a bug under a microscope—a new kind of species no one can figure out. "You really don't find any of those guys attractive?"

"Nope, not a single one of them." A little white lie never hurt anything, right? "I prefer brains over brawn."

"That's a pretty blanket statement don't you think? I bet a lot of them are smart." Peyton doesn't hold the same grudge as I do. She figured it was a few bad apples on our high school football team who persecuted Jacob until his suicide, not every jock in the world. I don't forgive as easily. Maybe it's the social worker in her. She sees the world through a different lens, and that's her right.

"Yeah, probably." I shrug. She's right, but it doesn't matter. I'm not going to hold it against her if she wants to date a player.

She grins. "What about Landon Brooks?"

A chunk of granola lodges in my throat and I try not to react, try not to let my eyes bulge out of my brain as I choke. Reacting will only fuel her ridiculous fantasy that Landon and I would be good together. She's wrong, a million times over. A trillion, even.

I snatch a juice box from my backpack, rip the straw open and jab the foil opening. After a big sip, I roll my eyes. "Oh, Please, Landon's ego is as big as—"

"His cock?"

Ohmigod.

My granola bar jumps back into my throat and I take another huge sip. In my calmest voice, I stare at her and say, "That is not what I was going to say. I mean, come on. I have no idea how big his...his thing is, and I don't want to know."

"His *thing*." She laughs. "Oh, come on, Ella. You can say cock. I know you've watched porn before. We've watched it together, for God's sake. We all have fantasies, and that's normal."

Flustered, I say, "Okay, fine. His cock. That's the last time you're going to hear that word on my lips, and the last time I'm going to think about it." It's possible that's a lie. I might actually think of it tonight—when I watch porn.

"His cock is going nowhere near your lips then?"

I plant one hand on my hip and glare at her as she teases and twists my words. "How many ways do you need me to say it, Peyton?"

She braces her hands on the bench behind her and leans back, lifting her face to the sun. "I can tell you like him."

"I do not like him."

"What do you have against him anyway?"

Oh, other than the fact that he's living rent free in my head, nothing. "He's an asshole, and wait, why did you say his ego was as big as his cock. How do you know that?"

She gives me a slow grin that says she knows me too well. "Ah, look at that, you are thinking about his *thing* again." She wags her dark brows. "You know, they just don't call him Torpedo because he's lightning fast, on the field. It's because he has a big—"

"Stop," I say. I take a fast breath. *Do not think about Landon's torpedo*. I'm two seconds from demoting her to the bleachers, when she sits up straight, her mouth gaping. "What?" I ask, my blood draining to my toes even though I have no idea what's going on. I only know that look on her face and it's bad. So very, very bad. She looks past my shoulder and points her finger.

"Uh..."

Ohmigod. I mouth the words, "He's behind me, isn't he?"

As she gives a slow nod, I spin around. Landon is adjusting his helmet as his gaze moves over my face. He's not smirking, or showing any sign that he overheard us. Thank God!

"Hey," he says and my stupid ovaries quiver as my gaze lands on his brutally handsome face. He's not typically handsome, with a square jaw, perfect skin, perfect features. No. He's a bit harder, his face scarred from fights, and football. It only makes him hotter.

"Hey," I squeak out.

He smiles at me, then looks past my shoulder to Peyton when she clears her throat. "Hey, Peyton."

"Landon," Peyton says. "Looking good out there."

He turns his attention back to me. "Coach wants to know if you've got this thing all figured out." He gestures with a nod to the camcorder and I try not to react to his sexy Texas accent. "You know how to work all these buttons?"

"Yes, I do," I say, and while I get that he has no idea how to use the camcorder, there are plenty of buttons this guy knows how to press. Yes, I'm talking about the buttons between a girl's legs and the ones on the end of each breast. I've heard the rumors, and have zero intentions of ever finding out if they're true. I'd have a better chance of landing an assistant director position with Spielberg right out of college than this guy has of landing a position between my sheets. Not that he wants that, but chances of either of them happening: zero.

His gaze rakes over me, and my goddamn legs nearly give out as those dark eyes ignite my blood from simmer to inferno. What the hell is wrong with me? I do not like football players. I do not like Landon.

Yeah, you just keep telling yourself that, Ella.

"Wait, am I seeing double," he asks, and looks from me to Ivy and back to me again.

"Ivy is my twin," I say with an exaggerated sigh, and steal a fast glance at her across the field. As if feeling my eyes on her, her head lifts, and she stares at me. I can't see her expression from where I'm standing. I can only imagine she's in shock to see me talking with Landon. Not because I don't associate with football players, but because a nerd like me would never be worthy of his attention. She has nothing to worry about. He's all hers.

Have at him, sis.

"How come I've never seen you around before?" He shifts from one foot to the other, and I become acutely aware of his height, and of the way his muscles fill out his uniform. Does he even need all that padding? The fresh scent of soap, fabric softener, and something uniquely Landon fills my senses. It's not a bad scent. Nope, not bad at all. Which really sucks.

"I hang in different circles," I tell him and like the nerd I am, I snort, and tap the camcorder. "Cinematography."

"Oh yeah?" Dark eyes leave mine to steal a quick glance at the camcorder, and for a second he almost seems truly interested. "You're one of those audio/visual students?"

I nod and resist the urge to roll my eyes, because honestly, the fact that he doesn't know what my major is called isn't his fault. I don't know a thing about football, and I kind of get the sense he's trying to be nice, although for the life of me I can't figure out why. I'm pretty sure he's not trying to lure me to the locker room so the team can beat the crap out of me, like those boys in high school did to Jacob.

"You mean nerds?" I ask, with a raised brow, and Peyton kicks my ankle. I whimper, but don't take my eyes off Landon. God, he's so alluring, his face brutally interesting, I'm not sure I can.

Something passes over his dark eyes. A hint of sadness? I'm not sure why I suddenly feel like I've bruised him somehow. Jeez, I'd never purposely hurt anyone, whether I liked them or not.

"I never said that. I just mean..." He shrugs one of those broad shoulders and it's all I can do to keep my gaze from dropping...from admiring all his muscles. "You, uh, you like movies, huh?"

"Yes. I like movies," I respond, and resist the urge to walk through the door he just opened. Once someone brings up movies, I could go on and on about films, rambling about what I like, what I don't like, but I don't want to bore him to death. He has a game to play, women to impress.

He rubs a scar beneath his eye, and it flares red. "Seen anything good lately?"

How did he get that? Football, or something else? "Yes," I say again, and he smiles.

"Any recommendations?"

Porn.

What. The. Hell.

Get yourself together, girl!!

"Depends on what you like." I say, trying for casual when my stupid brain is conjuring up all kinds of unwanted images. Landon on top of me, underneath me...

"You should come to the party tonight." He gestures to the field with a nod. "I'll show you what I like."

Holy shit, no. He is definitely barking up the wrong tree here. I am not one of his groupies, bunnies, cleat chasers, or whatever the hell they call women who sleep with footballers. Wait! My brain takes a moment to catch up, alerting me that the guy everyone calls torpedo—and not just because he's lightning fast—invited me to a party. Did I just enter the twilight zone or something? I think I might have heard him wrong.

"I'm busy," I say.

This time his smile is cocky, full of brazen confidence, and I get it. I really do. I get why women hand their panties over. "Come on, you can't be too busy to celebrate our win?"

"Pretty sure of yourself," I say in a bored voice, even though there's a storm going on inside me.

He cocks his head. "Attitude is half the battle, don't you think?"

"You don't want to know what I think," I mumble.

He grins, and despite myself, my stupid lips twitch. God, why am I acting like a dim-witted moth around him? Yes, he's a shining star and has his own gravitational pull, but I am not into egotistical football players. My only goal is to keep my head down, finish my degree and get a job in Hollywood. Why I'm suddenly on this guy's radar is beyond me. Did he lose a bet or something? Have to talk to the nerdy girl? If not, and if there's something about me that appeals to him, he should go after Ivy. We look alike, except she dyes her hair blonde, and he could have her with a snap of his fingers.

"Her name is Ella," Peyton says. "She'll be at that party."

I spin, and give my former best friend the death glare. She studies her nails, like she doesn't have a care in the world. From across the field, a whistle blows, and I nearly jump ten feet in the air when a big, strong hand lands on my arm. I spin to face Landon, and he snatches his hand back.

"Sorry, didn't mean to touch without permission." He holds both hands up, palms out. "I just ah, I gotta go. Coach is calling." He pauses for a brief second.

"What?" I ask as I reposition myself at the camcorder and reach for the record button. Wait, why is it on? Rattled, and pretending not to be, as Landon continues to stand there, six feet of sex in a football outfit, looming over my small frame, I flick the record button off, and close my eyes, hoping when I open them again, he'll be gone.

"Aren't you going to say good luck?"

Nope not gone, and goddamn that cocky grin of his. I'm going to give my traitorous body—one spot in particular—a good hard lecture when we get home. With my vibrator.

"Good luck," I murmur, sounding uninterested.

He backs up an inch and I can almost fully refill my lungs again. "See you tonight, Ella."

"Not going to be there," I say.

He pauses and I sigh as I look at him. Why won't he leave already?

"How about this? If I score a touchdown, you come, if I don't...then it's my loss. In more ways than one."

His loss? Okay, I really am in some alternate universe. Football players do not flirt with me, and that's the way I like it.

"Why would I bargain with you? What could possibly be in it for me?"

"Come tonight." He flashes perfect white teeth. "Find out."

"We'll be there," Peyton says, finality in her tone, letting us both know it's going to happen and the conversation is over.

"We will not be there," I clarify through clenched teeth. We have a better chance of getting snow in Southern California this late September evening. Not. Going. To. Happen.

"See you tonight, Peyton," Landon says. "See you too, Ella." He points to the camera. "Now you'd better press record. You don't want to miss my touchdown."

My God, could the guy be any hotter...I mean, cockier. Yeah, cockier, that's what I meant. The guy is *not* hot. Nope not hot at all.

Much.

If you want to see what kind of trouble Ella and Landon get into, check it out here **Fair Play.**

Hands On

Hands On

Body Contact

Full Exposure

Dossier

Private Reserve

House Rules

Under Pressure

Big Catch

Brazilian Fantasy

Improper Proposal

Boys of Beachville

Good at Being Bad

Igniting the Bad Boy

Bad Girl Therapy

Stone Cliff Series:

Crashing Down

Wasted Summer

Love Lessons

Wrapped Up

Eternal Pleasure Series

Instinctive

Impulsive

Indulgent

Sun Stroked Series

Seaside Seduction

Deep Desire

Private Pleasure

Captured and Claimed Series:

Yours to Take

Yours to Teach

Yours to Keep

Firefighter Heat Series

Fever

Siren

Flash Fire

Playing For Keeps Series

Slow Ride

Wild Ride

Sweet Ride

Breaking the Rules:

Hold Me Down Hard

Pin Me Up Proper

Tie Me Down Tight

Stand Alone Title:

Hands on with the CEO

Torn Between Two Brothers

Holiday Spirit

Unleashed

Knocking on Demon's Door

Web of Desire

ABOUT CATHRYN

New York Times and *USA today* Bestselling author, Cathryn is a wife, mom, sister, daughter, and friend. She loves dogs, sunny weather, anything chocolate (she never says no to a brownie) pizza and red wine. She has two teenagers who keep her busy with their never ending activities, and a husband who is convinced he can turn her into a mixed martial arts fan. Cathryn can never find balance in her life, is always trying to find time to go to the gym, can never keep up with emails, Facebook or Twitter and tries to write page-turning books that her readers will love.

Connect with Cathryn:
Newsletter https://app.mailerlite.com/webforms/landing/c1f8n1
Twitter: https://twitter.com/writercatfox
Facebook: https://www.facebook.com/AuthorCathrynFox?ref=hl
Blog: http://cathrynfox.com/blog/
Goodreads: https://www.goodreads.com/author/show/91799.Cathryn_Fox

Pinterest http://www.pinterest.com/catkalen/